The Wrong One

Carol Otis Hurst

Houghton Mifflin Company Boston 2003

Walter Lorraine Books

For the real Jesse and Keith
And Rebecca and Karl as well

Walter Lorraine (wn) Books

Copyright © 2003 by Carol Otis Hurst

www.houghtonmifflinbooks.com

Library of Congress Cataloging-in-Publication Data

Hurst, Carol Otis.
  The wrong one / Carol Otis Hurst.
    p. cm.
Summary: Kate and her brother Jesse are not happy when they
have to move from Brooklyn to an old house in Massachusetts
after the death of their father, but their newly adopted sister
from Korea quickly makes friends with a "blue lady" who
helps the family find a way to stay where they belong.
  ISBN 0-618-27599-1
[1. Moving, Household—Fiction. 2. Brothers and sisters—
Fiction. 3. Ghosts—Fiction.] I. Title.
  PZ7.H95678 Wr 2003
  [Fic]—dc21
                                        2002010511

Printed in the United States of America
QUM 10 9 8 7 6 5 4 3 2 1

The Wrong One

1

Ee-guh Aniya

"Nooo!" Sookan screamed. "*Ee-guh aniya!*"

Kate and Jesse Spencer stared at each other as their five-year-old sister waved her arms around wildly and took off down the hall as fast as she could go.

They'd never heard Sookan scream before. Even right after she came to them and woke up in the night confused and frightened, Sookan didn't scream. She hardly ever even cried.

They'd been choosing bedrooms in the house, and when they got to the one Sookan was to have, she took one look inside and screamed. By the time Kate and Jesse recovered from the shock and followed her down the hall, Sookan was sitting beneath the stained glass window on the landing halfway down the stairs with their mother patting her gently on the back.

"Sookan, dear," Mrs. Spencer was saying as she reached into her pocket for a Kleenex. "What is it, dear? Whatever is the matter?"

"Ee-guh aniya," Sookan said.

"Blow, dear."

Sookan blew.

"What does *ee-guh anita* mean, Sookan?" Kate asked. Kate was trying to learn to speak Korean. At eleven, an age she considered to be practically adult, Kate spent a lot of time thinking about possible careers for herself. For a while she had considered becoming a linguist—perhaps a translator at the UN, but picking up a new language was turning out to be lots harder than she had thought. Sookan's English was limited, but Sookan was picking it up much faster than any of them were learning Korean.

"Not *anita. Aniya! Ee-guh aniya!"* Sookan pointed back up the stairs. "Doll is *ee-guh aniya.*"

"Doll? What doll?" eight-year-old Jesse asked. "Did you see a doll, Kate?"

Kate shook her head. "Mom?" she asked.

"No, dear." Mrs. Spencer put her hands on Sookan's shoulders and turned her so that she could speak directly into her face. "The room is empty, Sookan. Remember? The movers wouldn't move anything into any of the rooms, although I certainly think there was no need to . . ." She trailed off, remembering the difficulties that morning.

The movers had started out amiably enough, but then Mrs. Spencer kept changing her mind about where things like the heavy library table should go. That's when they came up with the no-furniture-in-the-rooms rule.

"Anyway, there are no dolls in that room, Sookan, *ee-guh aniya* or not," she said.

"Yes!" Sookan insisted. "All over doll." She was clearly puzzled at their lack of understanding. *"Ee-guh aniya."*

"Well, don't cry, Sookan," Jesse said. He hated it when anybody cried, and lately there had been far too many tears all around. "Show me the dolls." He gestured for Sookan to come with him as he took a step back up the stairs.

"Noooooo!" Sookan wailed, turning back to her mother. *"Ee-guh aniya,"* she said, as if that explained everything.

"Well then, you come, Kate," Jesse said. "We'll search for *ee-guh* whatever."

Kate slowly followed him back to the room that was to have been Sookan's. Like all the other rooms in this old, dilapidated house, it was a mess. Paint hung in curls from parts of the ceiling while other areas displayed large stains in various shades of gray and brown. The yellowish paint around the windows was also cracked and peeling. The background of the wallpaper might once have been white but was now discolored to an uneven tan. The pattern on the wallpaper had little girls standing sideways in rows wearing wide skirts and bonnets that might have started out as pink.

"Pretty awful, isn't it, Kate?" Jesse leaped back and forth over the rolled-up carpet that stood kitty-corner across the bare floor, stirring up clouds of dust as he jumped. Like all the other floors in the house, this one had been painted battleship gray. That paint too was peeling back to reveal a previous layer of hideous dark brown.

"It's all awful," Kate agreed. "I hate it! I hate it! I hate it! I want to go home!" She kicked at the rolled-up carpet, releasing a bit of the anger and betrayal she'd been holding in all morning—as well as more clouds of dust. She was careful not to speak loudly enough for her mother or Sookan to hear, however.

"Yeah, me too," Jesse said softly. He stopped hopping and stood looking at the floor for a minute, then glanced around the room. "Don't think Sookan likes it much either, at least not this room. See any dolls?" He strolled around the room with his hands in his pockets.

"No!" Kate said. "There's nothing here but ugliness anywhere you look."

Jesse turned to leave and then moved closer to one wall. "Hey," he said, "maybe these figures on the wallpaper are dolls."

"Huh." Kate stepped over for a closer look. "Could be, I guess. Thought they were supposed to be girls, not dolls."

"Either way, they don't look like anything to be scared of. Wonder why Sookan's afraid of them," Jesse said.

"You think she's afraid?" Kate asked. She thought a moment. "More angry than afraid, I think. Who knows why. Maybe they remind her of something nasty in Korea." She touched one of the figures as if that would give her some answers, shook her head, and headed back to the landing. Jesse followed.

Mrs. Spencer was still comforting Sookan, who sat with her head down and shoulders slumped.

"Sookan," Jesse asked, "do you mean the dolls in the wallpaper?"

Sookan looked up. She nodded and smiled slightly, grateful to be understood at last. *"Ee-guh aniya,"* she said solemnly.

"There are dolls in the wallpaper? I didn't notice that," said their mother. "Well, if you don't like the wallpaper, Sookan, we'll just take it down and put up something you do like."

"Okay!" Sookan's mood changed instantly. She stood and pointed back up the stairs. "Do it!"

"Well, not this very minute, Sookan," said her mother. "We've got to get settled first. There's a lot to do. Just the cleaning is going to take time. It'll be a while before we can get to redecorating, dear." She gave a quick look around. "Quite a while."

Sookan's smile disappeared as she sat

7

back down on the stairs. *"Ee-guh aniya,"* she said.

Kate spoke before the tears could start again. "Hey, Sookan," she said. "Want to trade bedrooms?"

Sookan quickly looked up at her big sister, a wary look on her face.

Kate went on. "You can have my room and I'll take that one."

"Dolls?" Sookan asked suspiciously.

"No dolls," Kate guaranteed. "Just stripes and flowers—kinda sickly pink flowers."

"Okay!" Sookan said enthusiastically. She stood up and started down the stairs.

"Wait," Kate said. "Let's go make sure you like that room, Sookan."

"Nope," said Sookan. She headed out the front door. "I play."

"Oh, sure, Sookan," Jesse yelled after her. He picked up a carton and headed into the room that was to be his. "You just go and have a good time, Sookan. We'll take care of all the work." He grinned at his mother. "Kids today," he said. "No sense of responsibility at all."

2

Settling In

Once the problem of *ee-guh aniya* was solved, the settling in went smoothly enough—at least as smoothly as it could have under the circumstances. It was obvious that no one except maybe Sookan wanted to be here. Lots of "if onlys" were floating through their heads: if only their father hadn't died, if only there had been enough insurance to cover the mortgage on their Brooklyn home, if only this house wasn't such a dump.

As she swept out the bedroom with the doll wallpaper, Kate tried not to think about actually living here. Not that this room was any worse than the others. They were all awful.

She thought back to the life they had left behind. She'd just accepted it as the way things would be forever, or at least until she'd grown up and chosen her career—whatever that would be. Looking back on it now, it seemed that everybody was happy in Brooklyn. Her father had been a professor at Columbia University. Her mother had worked in graphic design for an advertising firm in Manhattan. Kate and Jesse had gone to the elementary school just a few blocks down the street. Life was convenient, easy, and pleasant.

The three-story brownstone house, the only home she and Jesse had ever known, was pretty and comfortable. Kate had loved her third-floor bedroom with its pale yellow wallpaper. Her best friend, Lizzie, had lived right next door. They were in the same class at school. They played together after school. They told each other everything. They'd waved to each other every night before they went to bed.

Jesse's friend Keith had lived across the street. The best bagel shop in Brooklyn was two blocks away. You could get Chinese food or pizza delivered at any hour of the day or night. Life was ordered and right in Brooklyn. Here in Massachusetts they had no friends; they were miles from every-thing, and there was ugliness everywhere Kate looked. She didn't know what to call this place. Certainly she'd never call it home.

Life had changed forever six months before, in the middle of a tennis game. One minute her father had been gloating over a good serve, and the next minute he col-lapsed on the court and died. The whole Spencer family's world had collapsed when he did.

As if that awful loss hadn't been enough, terrible decisions had to be made. There wouldn't be enough money to keep things as they had been. The family had to move somewhere less expensive. So their home on the tree-lined street had been sold, and they bought this old rundown house in western Massachusetts. It was miles from everywhere. There wasn't even a real town here, just roads and woods and occasional houses. Commuting to Manhattan was out of the question. Mrs. Spencer had quit her job there and planned to do free-lance work from here.

They had been going to cancel Sookan's adoption, which had been started just before Mr. Spencer's death. It didn't seem fair to bring a little girl halfway around the world to this grieving, fractured family. But then, neither did it seem fair to tell Sookan, who was waiting to be "processed" in an orphanage in Korea, that she didn't have a family waiting for her in America after all.

Months before, they had sent Sookan pictures of their family, carefully labeled to show who was who so that she'd recognize them when she came. They'd also sent a toy: a purple rabbit. In return they got a picture of Sookan, sitting on her bed, holding the purple rabbit in her arms and looking up at the camera with an expression on her face that made them all want to hug her immediately.

In the end, they'd gone ahead with the adoption, and that turned out to be the best decision they could have made. Everyone loved Sookan, and she was ready to return the love. Many times she was the only cheerful note in an otherwise cheerless day.

Of course, Sookan had no great difficulty leaving the house in Brooklyn. She'd lived there only a few weeks. Once she found out that they were all going, she happily packed her things, grabbed Purple Rabbit, and climbed into the car—the only one not completely dissolved in tears as they drove out of the city.

Kate filled the dustpan with its fourth load of debris and dumped it into the cardboard box in the hall that was serving as a temporary wastebasket. She looked around the room at the results of her efforts—

cleaner maybe, but not by much. The whole room still looked dingy and smelled moldy.

She turned as her mother spoke from the doorway. "Much better, dear," Mrs. Spencer said in that bright, phony tone she'd been using a lot lately. She stepped into the room and walked quickly over to the windows. "Oh, Kate," she gushed. "You've got a wonderful view of the pond. We can put your desk right here, and you can watch the birds as you do your homework and write your stories."

Kate was about to point out that it would be hard to write while looking out a window at birds, but she didn't think this was the time for such comments. Her mother was on a make-the-best-of-everything kick, and Kate knew from previous experience that it was better to let the mood run its course. Her mother was as miserable as she and Jesse were about all this. Kate had heard her crying quietly more than one night after everyone else had gone to bed.

"Yeah. It'll be great," Kate said, but she couldn't make it sound as though she meant it.

With a cheerful wave, her mother went on down the hall, and Kate went back to moving in. She shook her head as she heard her mother with Jesse in his room.

"Oh, Jesse," her mother was saying in that same phony voice, "you can hang your airplane models right in the center of the ceiling, and they won't bang into my head like they . . . They won't bang into my head."

Kate looked at the floor, wondering if the rug would be big enough to cover most of it. Whoever could have thought that a floor should be painted that ugly gray anyway? Floors should be the way they were in Brooklyn, polished hardwood with pretty scatter rugs carefully placed on them.

Angrily, she pulled and pushed her desk into the room and shoved it between the windows. She looked out on the pond, grinning in spite of herself at the thought of watching birds and writing stories at the same time. She did like bird watching and had begun a life list of her sightings. She was considering either ornithology or writing as a possible career.

Kate took her writing quite seriously. She had belonged to a writers' group in Brooklyn. Most of her stories were about Dirk Blood, her very tough, very clever detective hero, who operated out of an office in Los Angeles. Kate had never been to Los Angeles, of course, but she didn't see how that mattered. One of the detectives in her father's books "operated out of an office in Los Angeles."

Miss Goodman, who led the writers' group back in Brooklyn, had read some of Kate's stories and said they were remarkable although a bit gory. Miss Goodman had asked if Kate spent a lot of time watching TV. Kate didn't think she watched too much TV. She read a lot, though, especially her father's mystery books. She liked them much better than the mysteries written for kids, even if she didn't understand some parts.

Kate went into the hall and looked at the array of boxes. She found one labeled "Kate." Under a stack of dishtowels and her mother's knitting needles was the picture of Sookan on her bed in Korea. Kate had to smile when she looked at it. Sookan was a great kid, and Kate was glad she was with them, even though this was an awful place to bring her.

Kate looked closer at the picture. There was a reflection of a blue light on the wall beside Sookan that she'd never noticed before. She shrugged and put the snapshot with the dishtowels and needles on top of one of the other boxes. She brought the box containing her stories and bird list into her room and put it all in the bottom drawers of the desk. She didn't think she'd ever be able to look at any of them again.

She went outside to find Jesse and Sookan. They'd found a swing hanging from the maple tree in the side yard. Jesse sat on it and began to pump. Sookan watched, rubbing Purple Rabbit's ears, as Kate pushed him halfheartedly.

"Finished unpacking?" Jesse asked over his shoulder.

Kate nodded and kept pushing. She hadn't really, but she didn't want to unpack everything. That would mean that they were staying here, and that just wasn't going to happen. Somehow, some way, she'd get them all back to Brooklyn where they belonged. She pushed again. Sookan cackled with delight.

Seeing Sookan's interest, Jesse began to pump harder. "Hey! This is cool, Sookan! Look how high I can go! Push harder, Kate." He stretched his legs and tried to touch a thick branch each time the swing went up. "Harder!"

Sookan jumped up and began to push too. When the rope jerked, Jesse had finally had enough, and Sookan climbed on.

"My turn. No push," she said, holding tightly to Purple Rabbit with one hand and the rope with the other. So Kate and Jesse sat on the ground nearby, pulling up small clumps of grass and absent-mindedly tossing them at each other while Sookan happily wiggled her legs to make the swing twist first one way and then the other.

3

The First One

"Where's Sookan?" Kate asked the next morning as she stood at the kitchen window munching a donut. Even the outside of this place was ugly. A badly neglected stretch of lawn made up the back yard. There was a patch of scraggly woods at the end of it. To the right was the pond with an old barn beside it. This place must once have been a farm, but it sure didn't look like the ones she'd seen in books. A real farm might have been fun to live on, she thought. Maybe she could have become a farmer. Baby animals were cute, but she didn't think she liked the big ones so much.

Jesse took a sip of his milk. "Last time I saw her she was on the swing, talking a mile a minute."

"To Purple Rabbit, probably," Kate said.

She turned to look at her brother and wondered how he could drink that milk. It was thick with crumbs from the donut he'd crumbled into it.

"Nope! Doesn't have it with her," he said. He sipped some more milk through gritted teeth, then spooned some soggy donut crumbs into his mouth.

They were taking a break from unpacking and cleaning. Jesse and their mother were seated in something she called the breakfast nook. Jesse had asked where the lunch and dinner nooks were, but nobody seemed interested enough to answer. The cracked leather seat curved around like a booth in a restaurant at one side of the kitchen. Their mother had said this part of the room must have been added on to the house sometime in the fifties. Whether she meant 1850 or 1950 wasn't clear. Kate thought it could even have been 1750. This place was old.

Mrs. Spencer looked up.

"Purple Rabbit's on Sookan's bed in her room—her doll-less room." She smiled at Kate. "Thanks for that, dear." She looked out the window to see Sookan running toward the woods. "She does seem to be talking to someone. Maybe she has an imaginary friend." She turned toward Kate. "You had one, Kate. Do you remember? Her name was Mrs. Minipat, and we had to make a place for her at the table. I remember one time when your father—"

"Ever hear her talking to an imaginary friend before we got here?" Kate interrupted. She didn't want to hear about the cute things she had done when she was three, and she certainly didn't want to hear anything about her father. Not now.

Jesse wiped his mouth on the back of his sleeve as he took his dishes to the sink. "C'mon, Kate," he said. "Let's go explore the barn."

"Oh, yes." Their mother stood and began to clear the table. "Do go and explore, kids.

As soon as the telephone people get here, I've got to set up the computer and the fax machine. I'll call you when it's time to get back to work." She was fixing up an office in a room off the living room.

Glad to get out of the depressing house, Kate followed Jesse out the door and headed toward the barn.

The barn's first story was fieldstone set in gray cement on top of which the wooden structure stood. The boards had once been painted red, but were now faded to streaky brown. Kate examined the foundation with the first real interest she'd shown in the whole place. Rocks like these sometimes contained chiastolite crystals. She'd seen some on a field trip. Kate knew quite a bit about rocks. In fact, if writing or ornithology didn't pan out, she thought a career in mineralogy might be interesting.

Jesse opened the big barn door. It scraped along the dirt driveway as it swung out, sticking and then wobbling dangerously several times on the rocks in its path.

Even with the door wide open, it was dim inside the barn, the few windows too dirty to let in much light. Somebody must once have kept horses here. There were several stalls against the back wall. Jesse crossed the dirt floor and headed up the rickety flight of stairs to the upper levels of the barn.

"Be careful, Jesse," Kate said.

"C'mon, Kate! Let's see what's up here."

"Not me," Kate said. "I can't see well enough in here to look for the crystals. I'm going back for a flashlight."

It took a while to locate the flashlight. The box that was labeled "Tools" held books and silverware. Several boxes were labeled "Books," but at least one of those contained dishes. The box where Kate finally found the flashlight was labeled "Miscellaneous." So was a different box containing the magnifying glass. Kate looked at the other boxes in the downstairs hall. Her mother had printed "Miscellaneous" on most of them, except for one labeled "Things." Kate grinned. Organization was never her mother's strong point.

Sookan followed Kate back to the barn.

"Hey, Sookan," Kate said as she began a systematic search of the inside foundation, "see if you can find any crystals in these rocks. Chiastolites look like four-leaf clovers in stone."

Sookan looked at her sister for signs that she was kidding. Then she shook her head. "Nope," she said. "Gotta hunt." She headed over to the stall in the farthest corner of the barn and began poking into the dusty wooden boxes along the wall there.

They ignored each other for a while, each intent on her own search.

"Hey, guys!" Jesse called from the top of the stairs. "There's all kinds of cool stuff up here! Look what I found in the rafters!"

Kate shone the flashlight up the stairs to where her brother leaned over the rail.

"Look at you!" she said. "You're a mess! Are those spider webs in your hair?"

Jesse brushed at his hair with one hand as he came down the stairs. He thrust a dirt-covered object toward Kate.

"Never mind my hair," he said. "Take a look at this."

Sookan looked over from the corner of the barn. *"Ee-guh aniya!"* she yelled and took off out of the barn.

Kate and Jesse watched her round the corner of the house at full speed.

"Ee-guh aniya? What does that mean?" Jesse asked. "Is she talking about me or this?"

Kate looked down at the doll in his hand.

"Yeccch! Either way, it probably means dirty, disgusting thing," she said. "Throw it away, Jesse. You don't know where it's been."

"Sure I do," he said. "It's been up under the barn roof. I'm going to clean it up and see what it looks like underneath the guck." He headed back toward the house.

"Well, clean yourself up while you're at it," Kate said. She turned off the flashlight and followed him inside.

Jesse was filling the sink with water when Mrs. Spencer came in.

"What about spaghetti for sup—Freeze, Jesse!" she yelled.

Jesse froze, the doll just above the water in one hand, the dishwashing liquid in the other.

Both children watched warily as their mother tiptoed over to Jesse. She gently took the doll out of his hand.

"Oh, my," she said, lightly touching the doll's face with her index finger. "Will you look at that."

"Cool, isn't it?" Jesse said. "I found it in the barn. I'm going to wash it up so we can—"

"No," said his mother, her eyes on the doll. "You are not." She looked over at Jesse. "It's old, Jesse," she said. "Maybe very old. The body is cloth; only the head, arms, and legs are wooden, see? Water would destroy it."

"But it might be valuable, Mom," he protested. "I can maybe sell it at school if I clean it up. Betsy Shute will buy anything." He stopped. Betsy was at the old school. "Well, maybe the kids in the new school will buy it."

"You're not going to put this doll in water, Jesse."

"How do I clean it, then?" he asked.

"You don't," she said. "That's how a lot of antiques get ruined. I'll send it to Mr. Jacobinski in Br—" She stopped and then began again. "I'll send it to Mr. Jacobinski. He'll know how to clean it. In the meantime, Jesse, clean yourself up. And change your clothes while you're at it."

"No point in washing up yet," Jesse said as he headed for the door. "I'm going back to the barn. There may be more treasures up there."

"Are you really going to send that disgusting thing to an antique dealer?" Kate asked.

"Certainly," her mother said. "I don't know much about old dolls, but some of them are quite valuable. Mr. Jacobinski will know, or he can give us the name of someone who does. Heaven knows we could do with a little cash right now."

Kate began chewing the side of her thumbnail. "But I thought, with the move and everything," she said between nibbles. "I thought we'd have enough money now."

"Oh, we'll be fine, Kate," said her mother. "It's just that the computer and scanner and stuff cost a lot. I'd always used the company equipment before. Now I've got to have my own. Then there's the wallpaper and the paint. I hadn't thought about those things." She smiled and hugged her daughter. "It's expensive, that's all. It'll be okay, Kate."

But Kate's imagination was up and

running. What if they lost this house too? It was an awful place but better than nothing. Why, they could be homeless. They'd have to beg for money on the street. Forget about a career in mineralogy, writing or bird watching. They'd all have to become beggars. She pictured herself with Jesse and Sookan, holding their threadbare coats with no buttons closed about them with one hand while they held out cups to heartless passersby with the other hand.

"We're going to be all right, Kate," her mother said. "It's just that there's no money coming in from the business yet, so money's really tight right now. Once the business gets rolling, we'll be fine." She began to sing. *"Oh we ain't got a barrel of mo-ney, maybe we're ragged and fun-ny."*

"Good," Kate said quickly. Her mother had an endless supply of old songs in her head for every occasion and would sing the whole thing if you didn't stop her. Kate hadn't heard their mother do it since their

31

father's death, but it could drive you crazy. "It would be cold with no buttons on our coats," she said, closing the door behind her as she followed Jesse back out to the barn.

"Buttons?" asked her mother, stopping her song mid-note. "There's a whole box of buttons in one of these cartons. Try the one labeled 'Miscellaneous.'" Mrs. Spencer looked around to find herself alone in the kitchen. "Look at me, talking to myself. I'm as bad as Sookan."

4

A Visitor

There wasn't much time for treasure hunting in the barn or anywhere else during the next few weeks. School took up most of the kids' time, and setting up the office kept their mother busy. Sookan went to kindergarten, riding proudly on the bus with Kate and Jesse each morning and returning on the kindergarten bus at noon. She was making friends and picking up English quickly.

It was harder for Kate and Jesse. Most of the kids in their classes had been together for years. While they didn't go out of their way to be mean, neither did they seem eager to make friends with the new kids in town. Mostly they ignored both Jesse and Kate.

The teachers were nice enough, and the

work was just about what they'd left behind in Brooklyn. That was a relief, since both of them had been good students.

Although they took comfort in spotting each other in the cafeteria or playground, each was careful not to embarrass the other by speaking at such times. A nod or hidden wave had to do.

For the most part, the rest of the time was spent fixing up the house. Every Saturday morning Mrs. Spencer chose a room for a complete cleaning, and they all had to pitch in scrubbing everything, and then scraping paint and removing wallpaper.

After each room met Mrs. Spencer's tough standards, redecorating became the weekend project. The living room was full of wallpaper books, paint samples, and drapery swatches. There was no question that the house was looking better, but it didn't seem to change anyone's feelings about the place.

The front door had been painted with several coats of dark brown, and they used lots of paint remover and elbow grease to get at the natural oak beneath the brown and three other layers of paint, all of which were ugly. The knocker proved to be brass, and once they got the tarnish and dirt off, even Kate had to admit that it looked pretty good. Everybody took a turn with the brass polish while putting up with several renditions of their mother's song as they worked.

"I cleaned the windows and I swept the floor, and I polished up the handle of the big front door." The children rolled their eyes, but when the last coat of polyurethane went on the door, and the last application of polish was rubbed on the brass knocker, they all joined in with *"I polished up that handle so carefully that now I am the ruler of the Queen's Navy."*

When even a rented wallpaper steamer failed to remove the doll wallpaper in

Kate's room, they had to paper over it. Kate was relieved when the last bit of old wallpaper was covered. She didn't hate the pattern the way Sookan did, of course, but something about those rows of dolls did get to her. The new wallpaper had scattered roses against a white background, and going to bed surrounded by roses seemed easier.

Kate still missed her third-floor bedroom in Brooklyn. She looked out of the window each night before she went to bed, but there was no Lizzie waving back. At least the woodwork was gleaming white; the rose-colored curtains her mother had made lined but did not cover the windows. Kate tried not to look down at the ugly floor. The cracks in the ceiling had been painted over, but still showed through. In spite of herself, Kate had actually begun to watch birds and write stories again, though not at the same time.

She started a story in which Dirk Blood

still worked out of an office in Los Angeles, but she had him take a trip to Massachusetts to locate a suspect in an old wreck of a house there. Her bird watching had been successful too. She had added several birds to her count: an indigo bunting, a bluebird, and a hermit thrush.

Even with the new wallpaper, Sookan refused to go into Kate's room. She'd walk by on the other side of the hall, whispering *"ee-guh aniya"* under her breath.

One day they arrived home from school to find the doll all cleaned up, sitting on the table in the hall.

"Hey!" said Jesse, spotting it first. "The doll's back!" He peered closely at it. "And they put clothes on it. Wow! It looks like—"

"Nooooo!" screamed Sookan. *"Ee-guh aniya!"* She threw down her backpack and dashed back out the door.

Mrs. Spencer came rushing out of the office. "What is it?" she asked.

Jesse held up the doll. *"Ee-guh aniya,"* he said.

"Still?" his mother asked. "I thought maybe she'd like it now that it's cleaned up. Looks better, doesn't it?"

"It's kind of weird," said Kate, looking carefully at the doll. The painted eyes and eyelashes on the carved wooden face were faint, but she could make them out along with the tiny red circles on the doll's cheeks. Something about the face was unpleasant. The doll seemed to have an accusing look, as if they'd all done something wrong. The dress was pink, with the bonnet and muff a darker pink.

"It looks like the old wallpaper in Kate's room, doesn't it?" Jesse said.

"Why, so it does," said his mother.

"Well, Sookan sure saw it," Kate said, "and I don't think she likes it much."

"Put it in your room for now, Kate," said her mother. "There's no need to keep it out here if it upsets Sookan."

"Did Mr. Jacobinski tell you what it's worth?" Jesse asked.

"No, all he could do was clean and dress it. He said he didn't know enough about dolls to appraise it, but he thinks it might be a Queen Anne. He gave me the card of an antique-doll expert. It's on my desk somewhere. I'll take it there when I go to New York again."

"Valuable?" Kate asked.

"Could be." Mrs. Spencer smiled fondly at the doll. "If it's a Queen Anne, it could certainly tide us over this rough spot."

"Rough spot?" Kate asked. "Are we in a rough spot, Mom?"

"No, not really," Mrs. Spencer said. "We're getting by. Please don't worry so much, Kate. It's not your problem. That contract's bound to come through soon."

"Queen Anne, huh?" said Jesse, changing the subject. "Doesn't look very queenly to me, even with clothes on. Was Queen Anne mean?"

"If it's a true Queen Anne," said his mother, "it was made around 1700. There are only a few of them in existence, so it would be worth a lot. Handle it carefully, Kate. Put it on your dresser for now, in the middle where it won't get knocked off."

"And keep your fingers crossed," said Jesse, following his sister up the stairs. "I could use a raise in my allowance." He stopped and thought a minute. "Heck, I could use an allowance." He continued on up the stairs.

Kate was playing Chutes and Ladders with Sookan on the living room floor. Kate thought this was the dullest game ever made, but Sookan loved it. She cheered when she landed on a ladder and pretended to cry every time she landed on a chute. Her mind on something else, Kate reached to move Sookan's piece instead of her own.

"Uh-huh," Sookan said, slapping Kate's hand lightly. *"Ee-guh aniya."*

Kate looked around for the doll, but Sookan was smiling as she pointed to the other game piece.

"Oh, sorry," Kate said. "Hey, Sookan, does *ee-guh aniya* mean—"

A knock at the front door interrupted her.

"Can you get that, Kate?" her mother shouted from the office.

An old woman stood on the doorstep. Not much taller than Kate, she wore a blue coat with darker blue hat and gloves. A bright blue feather in the hat curved down onto the woman's white hair. Her face was very wrinkled, but she had a pleasant look. Kate knew it was rude to stare, but the woman looked as if she had stepped out of an old movie. Did real people wear hats like that? And gloves? It wasn't even that cold out.

"It sounds and feels the same," the woman said, fingering the now shiny brass knocker.

Kate remembered her manners at last.

"May I help you?"

Jesse came up behind her. "The same as what?" he asked.

The woman smiled. "The same as it used to." She smiled at the children. "I grew up in this house. It's lovely to see some things haven't changed."

"Oh, it's changed a lot. You should have seen it when we first got here," Jesse said.

"Oh, dear," said their visitor, standing back to look at the badly peeling clapboards. "Had it fallen into disrepair? This is a house that should be loved." She looked back at the children. "You probably think I'm a silly old woman, but I couldn't pass by without stopping to see the house again. This knocker—"

She touched it again, then turned and looked back down the walk. "There used to be portulaca beds along that walk. And there was arborvitae here and here. I loved every inch of this place."

"You should have seen our house in Brooklyn," Kate said. "It was beautiful."

"Yeah," Jesse said. "There was a deli right down the street."

Their visitor smiled. "Have you lived here long?"

Before they could answer, their mother did, as she came into the hall behind them. "Just a few months." She held out her hand. "Ruth Spencer," she said, "and this is my daughter Kate, and my son Jesse. And this is"—she indicated Sookan, who was peering around the corner—"my younger daughter, Sookan."

"Agatha Paran," said the visitor, quickly removing the glove on her right hand before shaking hands with each of them.

Kate tried to picture her as a little girl wearing that hat and gloves.

"Come in," said Mrs. Spencer. "When did you live here?"

"Almost seventy years ago," Mrs. Paran said softly as she stepped into the hall.

"We haven't finished the redecorating yet," Mrs. Spencer said, "and we haven't

43

even begun on the outside work, but would you like to see the house?"

Mrs. Paran smiled. "Oh, very much!" She took off her other glove, pulling carefully on each finger to do so. "My father was a military man and so was my husband. I've lived in lots of places over the years, but this house is what I always think of as home."

Kate thought briefly about making a career for herself in the military. The uniform and the travel would be nice, but she didn't think she'd like the war part.

Sookan and Jesse went to watch TV. Kate accompanied the grown-ups on the tour of the house, and the woman talked nonstop. Every room seemed to remind her of something that she had to tell them about. She stopped at the stained glass window on the landing and took the time to look out of each square. The big blue rectangle in the middle got two looks. She grinned broadly and said, "Had to do that every morning for good luck." They went on up the stairs, and she continued with her comments and stories. This had been her playroom, and this is how it looked then. This was her brother's room. He'd been killed in the war.

Mrs. Spencer had a dust cloth in her hand and, as they went from room to room, she tried to clean some of the surfaces while Mrs. Paran's attention was elsewhere. She needn't have bothered. Their visitor wasn't looking for dust; she was remembering her childhood. Some of her stories were interesting, but she did go on and on. Kate found her attention wandering as they neared the end of the tour. She thought Agatha Paran might make a good character for one of her stories, though. She could be a suspect in one of Dirk Blood's cases. "Listen, sweetheart," Dirk would say. "Wearing gloves, eh? Thought you'd leave no fingerprints, did you? Where were you on the night of—"

Kate snapped back to attention as they stepped inside her room. Mrs. Paran was beaming, "Oh, this was my room."

"What was on the wallpaper?" Kate asked suddenly.

"The wallpaper?" The woman thought a moment. "It was yellow with blue flowers, I think. Why?"

"Just wondering," Kate said, losing interest again.

"Yes," Mrs. Paran said. "That's just what it was. I remember how glad I was the day my father put it up. I'd hated the old wallpaper. It had a lot of ladies in bonnets all over it."

Kate's eyes widened. How could that be? There had been no sign of the yellow wallpaper with blue flowers on it. If that wallpaper had gone on over the dolls, shouldn't it still be there?

Agatha Paran walked over to look out at the pond. "There were snapping turtles in the pond," she said. "My father pulled a big

46

one out of the water by its tail."

"Wow!" Kate said, "Snapping turtles! Guess we'd better not swim there."

"Maybe we'll just keep that news from Jesse for a while," her mother said, picturing her son dragging snapping turtles into the house by the tail.

Their visitor spotted the doll on the dresser and picked it up. "This is interesting. How did you come by it?"

"Jesse found it in the rafters of the barn," Kate said. "Let's hope it's a Queen Anne."

"I never spent much time in the barn," the woman said. She gave a quick shudder. "Too many spiders. Keep looking though."

"You don't think this is a Queen Anne?" Mrs. Spencer asked.

Mrs. Paran smiled and winked. "There may be better things to come."

"Better things?" Kate asked. "Where?"

"You never know," Agatha Paran said. "This house has lots of secrets. Get to know it better."

Mrs. Paran put the doll back on the dresser. They went back downstairs where she refused their offer of tea. She stepped out the door and then turned back.

"Uh," she said hesitantly. "I do hope you come to love this house as we all did. It's very special. Have you noticed"—she shook her head slightly—"anything strange about the house?"

"Strange?" said Mrs. Spencer. "What do you mean?"

Agatha Paran smiled apologetically. "Oh, it's silly, really," she said. "My father used to say the place was haunted. He said he was afraid to stay here when the rest of us were away. He was kidding, of course. He must have been. But there were some things we couldn't explain."

"What things?" Kate asked.

"Oh, just little things," Mrs. Paran said. "Nothing important. You know how it is. Your imagination gets going. Well, you know."

"Nothing strange happening here," said Mrs. Spencer. "Just lots of work." She laughed. "Maybe the ghosts are waiting for us to get settled."

The visitor turned toward Kate. "I know you don't think so now," she said, "but this is a really great place to live. It will feel like home soon. Give it a chance."

Kate smiled politely, but she knew better.

Mrs. Paran thanked them for their kindness and left, promising to stop by the next time she was in town.

Kate went in to tell Jesse and Sookan about Agatha Paran's reactions to the house. When she got to the part about the doll, Sookan stood up and left the room. *"Ee-guh aniya,"* she said, but at least she wasn't screaming.

"Weird," said Jesse, looking after her. "Sookan hates it, Mom's thrilled with it, and now some lady thinks there's something better somewhere. And her father thought the house was haunted. Cool!"

"Hey, Jesse," Kate said. "I think *ee-guh aniya* means 'wrong one.'"

"That's what Sookan's been yelling? 'Wrong one'?"

Kate nodded. "I think so." She told him about the Chutes and Ladders game.

"The doll's the wrong one?" Jesse said. "Is there a right one?"

"Beats me," said Kate. "Weird, isn't it?"

"Lotsa weird things going on," said Jesse. "This is getting good!"

And the next night the television went crazy.

5

Television Hijinks

Sookan was in bed. The others were watching a movie in the living room. The movie started out all right, but it was getting boring — lots of silly dancing and long conversations. Jesse quit and went up to his room after a few minutes.

A while later, Kate looked over just in time to see her mother's eyes close and her head slump. Mrs. Spencer woke herself with a jerk. "That's it for me, Kate," she said. "I'm going to bed. Don't forget to turn out the lights when it's over. I'll lock up."

Soon Kate gave up on the movie too. She was in the bathroom brushing her teeth when her mother said, "Kate, you didn't shut off the TV."

"Yes, I did, Mom," Kate said. She thought

a moment. "I'm sure I did." She stepped out into the hall.

"Well, listen," her mother said. "It's on."

Kate could hear the television voices.

"Sorry, Mom," she said, and headed back downstairs.

Kate pushed the off button firmly. The screen went black, and she turned to leave the room. There was a click, and the set came back on. Kate was reaching for the off button when she noticed that the movie was getting better — a car chase had begun.

"Action at last!" she thought, and sat down to watch it. Ten more minutes and the car chase and the movie were over. She clicked off the TV and waited a moment to make sure it didn't come on again. She stopped again to listen on the stairs. All was quiet. Grinning at her own foolishness, Kate went up to bed.

The next night Mrs. Spencer was watching the news with Tom Brokaw when Kate came into the room.

"Anything earthshaking going on?" Kate asked.

Her mother shook her head. "Must be a slow news day." She grabbed the remote and clicked off the TV. "What's up with you?"

"I've got to come up with a science proj—"

The television came on again. Mrs. Spencer frowned and picked up the remote. Pointing it directly at the set, she pushed the off button firmly. The screen went dark, and she turned back to her daughter.

"A science project. Hmm," she said. "Any—"

The set flickered on again.

"What on earth?" Mrs. Spencer murmured. Then she shrugged. "Remote must be broken," she said. She got up and pressed the off button on the set itself.

"It won't do any good," Kate said.

Even as she spoke and her mother sat down again, the TV came back on.

"Must be a loose wire," said her mother. "I'll unplug it."

"Just wait," Kate said. "Wait till the program's over."

"Why?"

"I don't know why," Kate said, "but you can't shut it off in the middle of a program."

"Well, that's ridiculous," said her mother. "The TV set doesn't know whether a program is over or not."

Kate shrugged. "Something does," she said.

Tom Brokaw said, "I'm Tom Brokaw. I'll see you here again tomorrow night," and Kate said, "Now, Mom. Shut it off."

Her mother did, and they waited. Nothing happened.

"Hey, Jesse! Sookan!" Kate yelled as her mother continued to stare at the screen. "Come here and see this!"

Jesse came halfway down the stairs, then climbed on the banister and slid the rest of the way down. "What's up?" he said when he landed.

Sookan came from the kitchen and stood in the doorway.

"Watch this," Kate said. "Do it, Mom."

With a nervous glance at her children, Mrs. Spencer pointed the remote at the set and clicked. A rerun of *Seinfeld* had just begun. She looked at Kate, who nodded, and she clicked it off.

"Gee, that's really great, Mom," Jesse said. "You can turn the set on and off."

The TV came back on.

Sookan giggled. For a second, Jesse's mouth dropped open.

"Very funny," he said. "You can't fool me. You're hitting the button with your hand. Turn it off, and put the remote down."

Kate grinned. "It won't matter. You can't shut it off in the middle of the program."

"Oh, sure," Jesse scoffed. "How stupid do you think I am? The TV can't tell if it's the middle."

"You'll see," Kate said.

Mrs. Spencer was just putting the remote on the table when *Seinfeld* came back on.

They all took turns with the remote, but no matter who clicked, the TV wouldn't stay off until they got to the commercial break. Then Jesse clicked and it stayed off. He stared at Kate.

"See?" she said, lifting her right eyebrow.

"Is *Seinfeld* the only program it likes?" Jesse asked.

"No," Kate said. "It likes old movies too."

"And the news," Mrs. Spencer added. She looked at Kate. "Is that what was going on the other night?"

"Yep," Kate said. "It wouldn't shut off until the movie was over. I thought it was my imagination."

"Is it only this TV that does it?" Jesse was already running up the stairs. "Let's see if it will work on another TV!"

Behind them, the television came on again as the commercials ended.

The others got to Jesse's room in time to see him turn on the old black-and-white set. They watched the second half of the first round of *Jeopardy*, and Jesse shut off the set. Nothing happened.

"Darn," Jesse said. "Guess it only works on the living room set."

Sookan continued to watch the blank screen. The others were leaving his room when the set came back on, just in time for Double Jeopardy.

"Why'd it wait?" Jesse asked.

"Guess it doesn't like commercials," his mother said. "A ghost after my own heart."

"A ghost?" Kate asked. "Do you think it's a ghost?"

"No," Mrs. Spencer said, "but there's something strange going on. I need more evidence before I declare us haunted." She was smiling a bit nervously.

"Watch it, Mom," Kate said. "The ghost may take that as a challenge."

"A ghost! We've got a ghost! Wait till I tell

the kids at school that I've seen a ghost!"
Jesse said.

"You haven't seen a ghost," Kate said.
"Nobody's seen a ghost."

Nobody paid any attention to Sookan, who was talking softly as the others left the room.

6

Pah-rahn Agah-si

Jesse brought a few kids home the next afternoon and charged them fifty cents to go through the house turning on and shutting off the TV sets. When the sets behaved just the way TV sets usually do, Jesse reluctantly refunded their money, and they all went off to the barn for a more interesting adventure. He took a lot of kidding, but the kids stayed around all afternoon.

One afternoon Kate and her mother were in the living room. Mrs. Spencer was searching through a computer manual. Kate was reading *The Big Sleep,* another of her father's mysteries. It was the first of those books she'd been able to bring herself to read since he died.

His thin, claw-like hands were folded

loosely on the rug, purple-nailed. A few locks of dry white hair clung to his scalp, like wild flowers fighting for life on a bare rock, Kate read. Pretty good stuff. She liked the image of thin, claw-like hands. Maybe she could use it in one of her stories.

Sookan was outside. Lately she seemed to have abandoned the barn search and was spending most of her time on the swing. She'd learned to pump, and she chatted away happily as she went back and forth.

Kate heard Jesse sliding down the stairs and said, "Hey, Jesse! Want to play Monopoly after I finish this chapter?"

Jesse's footsteps stopped just outside the living room. "What the—?"

Kate put the book down and went into the hallway. "What's up?" she asked.

"Look!" Jesse was pointing down the hall toward the kitchen.

"Mom," Kate called softly. Something in her tone brought Mrs. Spencer quickly into the hall.

Through the doorway, they could see a blue light moving around in the kitchen. With their mother in the lead, they all went into the kitchen. It was always colder there. Mrs. Spencer had said that this was because there was so little insulation in that part of the house. Now, however, it was more than cold—it was freezing.

As they stood there shivering, the blue light—darker in the center where it seemed almost black, and fading to white at the edges—hovered in the middle of the room. Then it moved to the wall, where it grew smaller, drawing itself inward until it was the size of a golf ball, and then, abruptly, it disappeared.

Kate walked over to the spot and put first one finger and then her whole palm on it.

"It's like ice," she said.

Jesse rubbed his hand on the spot and grinned. "Spooky, huh? You can't say we didn't see a ghost this time, Mom."

"We didn't see a ghost," said his mother.

"We saw a light."

"A ghost can be a light," Kate said.

"Can it?" Jesse asked. "How do you know that? Aren't ghosts supposed to look like see-through people?"

"I read it somewhere," Kate said. "Many ghosts appear as lights."

"It wasn't a ghost," Mrs. Spencer quietly insisted.

"It wasn't, huh," Kate said. "I suppose you're going to come up with some explanation for it. A blue light appears in the kitchen, turns the room cold, gets smaller, and disappears into the kitchen wall. And all that was caused by—?"

"Well." Her mother smiled a little nervously. "Well, there's blue glass in the stained glass window on the landing, right?"

"Right," Kate and Jesse said in unison. Since Agatha Paran's visit, they had begun looking through each color in the stained glass window, with two glances through the blue rectangle, every morning as they came downstairs. Now they folded their arms across their chests, waiting for the explanation. Kate raised her right eyebrow, and Jesse's face contorted as he tried to raise his.

"Well, the sunlight shines through that window and makes a blue shadow on the wall."

"Mom," said Jesse. "The wall across from the stained glass window is the hallway wall, not the kitchen wall. How does the blue light get to the kitchen?"

"From the mirror on the hallway wall, of course," Mrs. Spencer said quickly. You could tell she was making this up as she went along. "The reflection bounces off the mirror and into the kitchen." She smiled a little hesitantly.

"Where it gets smaller and turns the room colder?" Kate asked skeptically.

"That was just your imagination." Mrs. Spencer went back to the living room and picked up the computer manual. "Problem solved."

Kate looked at Jesse. "You believe that?" she asked.

"Nope," he said, "and I don't think she really does either."

A few weeks later Sookan and Kate were playing Chutes and Ladders again. Sookan was talking to herself, chuckling over the moves.

As usual when they played, Kate got bored quickly and was barely listening. She was plotting a new story. Dirk Blood would find a headless body with claw-like hands lying on the rug.

Sookan said, "It's not here."

"Hmmm? What's not here?" Kate asked.

"Not you. Pah-rahn Agah-si," Sookan said. She moved her piece on the board.

Kate grinned. "And who is Pah-rahn whatever?"

"Pah-rahn Agah-si," Sookan said. She

nodded toward the doorway as she shook the die for her next move.

In spite of herself, Kate looked toward the doorway. There was no one there.

"Uh, Sookan? Do you talk to Pah-rahn Agah-si a lot?"

"Yep," she said. "Your turn, Kate."

"You told Pah-rahn that something isn't here," Kate said. "What isn't here?"

"Doll," Sookan said, her eyes still on the board. "Your turn, Kate."

"Sookan," Kate said. "Never mind the game. Tell me about this person you talk to. Is it here with us now?"

Sookan looked toward the doorway and shook her head. "Nope," she said. "Gone now."

"Does that name mean anything or is it just a name?"

Sookan looked quickly around the room as if searching for something. Then she looked at the game board. She pointed to a blue space. "Pah-rahn," she said, tapping the board. Then she looked toward the office. "Agah-si," she said.

"Office?" Kate said. "Blue office?"

Sookan giggled. "Nope!" She got up and went into the office. A minute later she came out, dragging her mother by the hand. "Agah-si," she said, pointing to her.

"Blue mother?" Kate said. "You've been talking to a blue mother?"

Sookan giggled harder.

"Blue?" Mrs. Spencer said, looking down at the tan shirt and slacks she was wearing. "I'm not blue." She thought a minute. "Oh, you mean sad? I'm not sad, really, kids. I'm feeling quite cheerful today. I just got a lead on a new contract. I'm not at all blue."

Sookan just shook her head. Her eyes were twinkling as she pointed to herself, then to Kate, and then to her mother. "Agah-sis," she said.

"Blue people?" Kate asked.

With a shrug, Sookan gave up and went

back to the game. "Your turn," she said.

Mrs. Spencer waited a moment, but when they continued to ignore her, she went back into the office singing, *I want some red roses for a blue lady. Mr. Florist, take my order please.*

"Sookan," Kate asked, "do you really see this Pah-rahn Agah-si?"

Sookan looked around. "Not now. Your turn."

Kate was not about to be distracted. "But sometimes, Sookan, do you really see this blue whatever?"

Sookan shrugged and picked up the die and shook it. "Okay," she said. "My turn." She looked at the die as it landed on the board and moved her piece four spaces.

Kate suddenly remembered the picture of Sookan and the blue spot on the wall.

"Was Pah-rahn Agah-si with you in Korea, Sookan?"

Sookan grinned and nodded.

"Was Pah-rahn Agah-si in Brooklyn?"

Sookan thought a moment and then shook her head.

"But it's here. And it's looking for the doll?" Kate persisted.

"Yep!" Sookan looked up at her sister. "You playing?" she asked.

"Well," Kate said, intent on this conversation, "Pah-rahn Agah-si must not be looking very hard. The doll is right on my dresser."

Sookan shook her head and shivered. *"Ee-guh aniya,"* she said. "Your turn."

Kate gave up and shook the die.

Later, as they were picking up the game, Kate said, "Sookan. About that doll—"

"Ee-guh aniya," Sookan said again, and hurried out to the back yard.

When Jesse came in, Kate got the snapshot and cornered him in the living room. "Listen, Jesse," she said. "Sookan's imaginary friend is our blue light, I think. Look at the wall in this picture."

Jesse looked at it carefully. "There's a blue spot, all right. Never noticed it before." He thought a minute, then shook his head. "Nah," he said. "The blue light has never been around when Sookan's talking to the air. She's just got an imaginary friend like you did, you cute little thing."

"Quit it, Jesse," Kate said. "I think Sookan can see it when we can't. She says its name is Pah-rahn Agah-si, and that means blue something or other and, she says, it's looking for the doll."

"Not a very good looker, then, is it?" Jesse said. "Isn't it still on your dresser?"

Kate nodded.

"You'd think a ghost would know where everything in this house is," Jesse said. "Don't they walk through walls and things?" He grinned. "It sure knows where to find the TV sets."

"Have you been playing On and Off again?" Kate asked.

"Sometimes," he admitted. "The ghost likes *Wheel of Fortune*."

"Let's write them a fan letter and tell them," Kate said. "Dear Mr. Sajak, our ghost likes your program."

"We might get to meet Vanna," he said.

Kate went back to the subject. "Have you seen the blue light since that night in the kitchen?" she asked.

"No," he said slowly, "but some nights —" He paused.

"Go on," she said. "Some nights —"

"Some nights it gets really cold in my room," he said. "I wake up and I'm freezing. I put on more blankets until I'm practically buried in them, but it doesn't help." He watched his sister carefully to see how she was taking this. When she didn't laugh at him, he went on. "And sometimes when I go into the bathroom, it seems kinda blue in there. There's no blue light, really, but things look bluish, you know?"

Kate shook her head. "Nothing like that

in my room or in the bathroom when I'm there," she said, disappointed not to be able to add to the list of ghostly hijinks. Then she smiled. "Obviously Pah-rahn Agah-si doesn't go in my room. That's why it doesn't know where the doll is. Let's put the doll where it can find it."

"Where?"

"In the kitchen."

"We can't put it in the kitchen," Jesse said. "Sookan hates it. She'd never go in the kitchen again."

"We won't leave it," Kate said. "We'll just put it there for a few minutes while Sookan's outside. Just to see what happens."

"And what if the ghost takes it, Kate? What will we do then?" Jesse looked around to make sure their mother wasn't there. "Mom really needs the money from that doll, Kate. I think things are getting tough around here."

"Why?" said Kate, suddenly very anxious.

"What have you heard?"

"I heard her talking on the phone to someone from the bank yesterday," he said. "There's some problem with the mortgage, I think."

Kate chewed on her thumbnail and then said, "Well, if the ghost takes the doll, we'll just take it back."

"Oh, that I'd like to see," Jesse said. "You and the ghost fighting over a doll."

But Kate was already heading up the stairs. In a minute she was back bearing the doll.

"Where are you going with that?" asked their mother as they came into the kitchen.

"Sookan says the ghost is looking for it," Kate said. "So, we're putting it where Pah-rahn Agah-si can find it."

"Oh, no, you don't," their mother said, taking the doll out of her daughter's hands. "This doll is going to pay our bills. The ghost will just have to find her own doll. You take that right back upstairs."

"But Mom," Jesse said.

"No buts. Back it goes."

"So much for that idea," Jesse said as Kate returned the doll to her dresser. "What now?"

"Beats me," Kate said. "Mothers have no imagination, have you noticed?"

That night Kate went into the office to use the computer.

"Hey, Mom!" she called. "What's the doll doing in here?"

"The doll?" Mrs. Spencer went into the office. "I thought I told you kids to take it back to your room."

"You did and we did," said Kate. "So what's it doing in front of the computer? Looking for a chat room?"

"Jesse must have done it," Mrs. Spencer said. "Take it back upstairs, Kate."

"I'll bet Pah-rahn Agah-si did it, Mom. Better leave it here."

Mrs. Spencer shrugged. "Well," she said,

"I suppose it's safe enough here, but I do wish you kids would stop playing with it. Put it on the shelf where it won't get knocked off, Kate."

The next morning the doll was in front of the computer when Mrs. Spencer went into her office. She moved it to a big shelf on the side wall.

"Jesse," she called out as he was leaving for school. "Leave the doll alone."

Jesse looked blankly at his sisters and then shrugged as they all went out the door.

7

Measuring Mountains

"Nuts!" Jesse threw down his pencil and crumpled up the paper he'd been working on. "That won't work either."

Neither Kate nor Sookan looked up from her work at the dining room table. Kate was tracing the route of Vasco da Gama on a world map from the description of his voyage in her social studies book. Sookan was "reading." For her, that amounted to going through books and calling out the names and sounds of letters she knew.

"I can't do this. It's too hard," Jesse said. He threw the crumpled paper at Kate, who, without looking up from her map, crumpled the tossed paper tighter and threw it back at her brother.

"Well, don't blame me," she said.

Sookan looked at each of them and

giggled. She closed the book she was working with and put it back in the pile she'd pulled from the boxes upstairs. She picked up a crayon as she took out a large sheet of drawing paper, and began carefully drawing letters and shapes on the paper. She stuck her tongue out between her lips, as she often did when she was concentrating.

After a while, Sookan pushed the paper over to Kate. "What's it say?" she asked, pointing to a line of letters.

"Zbykkkld," Kate said.

Sookan shook her head, took the paper back, and worked some more.

"What's it say?" she asked, thrusting the paper in front of Kate again.

"O," Kate said.

"Says O?" Sookan asked, pleased to have printed something that seemed meaningful.

"Yep."

Sookan nodded, and they both went back to work.

"Now?" asked Sookan, shoving the paper back.

She had printed the letter H after the O.

Kate grinned. "Oh," she said, pushing it back.

"No," Sookan said. "Together now."

Kate nodded. "Oh," she repeated.

Sookan stared at the paper, turning it around in her hands. When she shoved it back at Kate, she had turned it upside down. "Says O?" she asked.

Kate smiled. "No," she said. "Now it says 'Ho.'"

Sookan looked at her suspiciously. She knew sometimes they kidded her, and she didn't always get the joke. Then she turned the paper upside down and pointed to a line of C's she had made.

"What's it say?" she asked.

"Ccccccc," Kate said.

Sookan pointed to the OH. "Say 'Oh' and 'Ho'?" She pointed to the line of C's. "Say nothing?"

"Yep. I know it's crazy, but that's how O's and H's work together, Sookan."

Sookan shook her head, turned the paper back around, and went on with her "work." Minutes later the paper was in front of Kate again. Sookan had printed "HO, HO, HO." "Santa Claus," she said.

She and Kate laughed, but Jesse sighed. "Kate," he said. "Help me. How do you figure out the height of a mountain?"

"Which mountain?" Kate asked.

"Any mountain."

"Well, do you mean Mount Everest or Mount Tom?"

"It doesn't matter."

"It does if you're climbing it," Kate said.

"I'm not going to climb it," Jesse said.

"Good thing it's not Everest," said Kate. "I'd never choose mountain climbing for a career. People lose fingers and toes on Mount Everest."

Sookan looked closely at her fingers. She bent each of them down and looked at her hand closely from the other side.

"I can't climb it," said Jesse.

"Of course not," said Kate. "You'd need special equipment. Pitons and ropes and things."

"Kate!" Jesse didn't think this was at all funny, but Kate was on a roll.

"And a Sherpa," she said. "You'd have to hire a Sherpa for a guide. I don't know what you'd do about oxygen. It'd be expensive. And then there's the plane ticket to Nepal. Where's the money coming from? Better start collecting empty bottles, Jesse."

"Very funny," Jesse said. "Quit kidding around, Kate. I need to come up with a way to measure a mountain."

"Well, how can you measure it if you don't know which mountain? I think you have to climb it and carry one of those altimeter things. Or maybe a tape measure. Hey, maybe you all could land right on top of it in a helicopter." Both Kate and Sookan were obviously enjoying this.

Jesse sighed. "Kate," he said, trying for patience, "I need to come up with a way to figure out how tall a mountain is. Any mountain," he added quickly, before Kate could start in, "without climbing it."

"Well," Kate said, "if you know the name of the mountain, you can look it up in the atlas."

"I can't use the atlas."

"I'll show you how. Is there an atlas in that pile, Sookan?"

"Kate," he said. "I know how to use an atlas. I just can't use it for this assignment. It's for math. We have to come up with a way to measure a mountain. Now, can you help me or not?"

"Use a yardstick?" Kate offered.

Jesse shot her a look and left the table. Kate shrugged at Sookan, and they both went back to work.

Kate was late coming down to breakfast

the next morning. Sookan was seated in the breakfast nook, eating Froot Loops and calling out the names of the letters on the cereal box. Their mother was sitting beside Sookan, reading the newspaper and drinking coffee.

Jesse called out from the dining room. "Hey! Cool! Thanks, Mom!"

"You're welcome, dear," she called back.

Jesse walked into the kitchen carrying an open book. "This is great!" he said. "I didn't even know we had a book like this."

"What book is that, dear?" Mrs. Spencer asked.

Jesse looked at her. "This one," he said. He showed her the title: *Far-Out Solutions*.

"Hmmm," said his mother, going back to her paper. "That's nice, dear."

"You mean you didn't leave this open on the dining room table?" Jesse asked

"No, dear," she said. "Is it good?"

"It gives the directions for measuring a mountain," he said.

"Which mountain?" asked his mother, her eyes still on the paper.

Jesse grabbed Kate's arm as she brushed by on the way to the refrigerator. "Kate?" he asked. "Did you do it?"

"Do what?" she asked, without much interest, as she took out the orange juice.

"Leave this book open on the dining room table."

Kate was slow at waking up in the morning and often a bit cranky. "If you don't like it open, close it," she said.

"Kate!" he said, grabbing her arm again.

"Quit it, Jesse! You'll make me spill this."

Jesse let go of her arm but held the book in front of her face. "Look at the page it's open to."

Kate looked. At the top of the page it said, "Solution #94: Measuring a Mountain." She stared at Jesse, who read it aloud:

"On a sunny day, put a three-foot-long stick into the ground. Measure the shadow cast by the stick. Take that number and divide it by three. Find the edge of the mountain's shadow. Estimate the distance between the shadow's edge and the center of the mountain. Divide that number by the number you got when you divided the stick's shadow by three. That figure is the approximate height of the mountain."

"That's very clever," Mrs. Spencer said. "Seems like a lot of work, though. Wouldn't it be easier to look it up in an atlas?"

"Mom!" Jesse said. "Where'd the book come from? Who put the book on the table? Who opened it to this page?"

"Not me," Kate said.

"Well, I didn't," said their mother.

They looked at Sookan, who grinned. "School time," she said. She carried her dishes to the sink, grabbed her backpack, and headed out the door.

Jesse looked after her. "Could she—?"

"Maybe it was Pah-rahn Agah-si," Kate said. She picked up her backpack and followed her sister out the door.

Jesse caught up to Kate at the bus stop. "Hey, Kate," he said. "Do you really think Pah-rahn Agah-si found the book?"

"Well," Kate said. "Mom says she didn't do it. Sookan is just learning her letters, so what do you think the chances are that she found the right book and then the right page in it?"

"Well, there's a diagram. Maybe Sookan saw the diagram and . . ." Jesse's voice trailed off. Then he began again. "If Pah-rahn Agah-si did it, can it find the answers to all my homework assignments? That'd be cool, wouldn't it, Kate? I'd just leave the problems on the table every night, and in the morning Pah-rahn Agah-si would have found the answers for me."

As they waited at the bus stop, Jesse was too excited to stand still. He hopped on and off the curb as the ideas spilled out.

"Hey!" he said. "This can be a money-maker, Kate. I can charge kids to have Pah-rahn Agah-si find the answers to any of their questions. We can make enough money to go back to Brooklyn."

"What happens if we don't have a book with the right answers in it?"

"You think that *Far-Out Solutions* is really our book? I never saw it before. Did you?" He tried to balance on the rim of the curb with one foot while the other waved in the air.

Kate stepped back to avoid getting hit by Jesse's flailing arms and shrugged. "I don't know. Probably. I know we packed up box after box of books. There were all kinds — Dad's, Mom's, yours, and mine. Sookan's books could fill a couple of boxes. You know how full the shelves were. We haven't got enough bookcases for them in this dumb house. Lots of them are still in boxes in the upstairs hall. It could have been in that pile Sookan had out, and it just happened to fall open to that page."

"Do you believe that?"

"No. Here comes the bus."

"There's gotta be a way to make money off of this," Jesse said, climbing on the bus behind his sisters. "A ghost that can find the answers to any questions has got to be worth something."

"You don't know that it can find answers to *any* questions," Kate pointed out. "If it was the ghost, it only found one answer to one question."

"That's right!" Jesse said. "I'll have to give it more questions. Wait till tonight!"

The next morning, while Kate and Sookan came into the kitchen for breakfast, Jesse was trying to explain to his mother why he hadn't done his homework.

"I did the math stuff. The ghost was supposed to find the answers to all these stupid science and social studies questions, Mom. Then all I'd have to do is copy them down."

"And?" she asked. "What happened?"

"Well, it may have found them but . . ."

"Looks like you've got a lot of reading to do," said his mother as they all followed Jesse into the dining room.

The entire surface of the dining room table was covered with open books: atlases, dictionaries, and textbooks.

Kate asked, "Did you—?"

"No!" Jesse said. "But how am I supposed to figure out which book has which answer? It'll take me a week."

"Don't panic," Kate said. "We've got time. We can probably find the answers on the Internet. Okay if we go online, Mom?" she called.

"Okay," her mother called back.

"Bring the questions, Jesse," Kate said. She led the way into the office. "Move the doll out of the way, and we'll give the key words in each question to the search engine."

"Thanks, Kate," Jesse said. He put the

doll on the shelf and turned back to his sister. "What's the population of Nome? Darn ghost," he muttered as Kate typed "Alaska, Nome, population."

"Yeah," Kate said as she waited for the search engine to find the references. "I hate an unreliable ghost."

Later, at the bus stop, Sookan was talking to the kids from down the road. Jesse came running out, stuffing a banana into his mouth. "Think this'll be all right?" he asked Kate as he handed her his paper.

She looked at it. "Mrs. Lutak'll never take this. It's a mess. There's an 'e' at the end of 'France,'" she said, "if you mean that scribble to be 'France.'" She handed it back.

"Darn!" he said. "Give me your pen."

He balanced a book and his paper on his knee and put in the "e."

"Hey, guys," he said as he got on the bus. "How do you spell Luxembourg?"

Jesse left only three questions for the ghost on the dining room table that night and did all his homework himself.

"No point in covering the table with books again," he said as they went upstairs for bed. "The secret is asking only a few questions at a time."

"I see," Kate said. "Good to know."

"Yeah." Jesse was taking off his sweatshirt as he headed toward the bathroom. "Took me a while to come up with three good ones. If this works, we have to think of a way to make money with it."

Kate grinned. "Maybe that should have been one of your questions."

"Kate!" Jesse was shaking Kate's shoulder the next morning. "Look at this!"

"Huh? What time is it?" Kate asked, opening one eye and reaching out for the alarm clock.

"Ten minutes to seven," he said. "You've

got to get up in ten minutes anyway. Look at this! The ghost answered a question!" He waved his paper in her face.

She grabbed it and then threw it back at Jesse. The whole paper was filled with O's and H's of many sizes and colors. "Ghost, my foot!" she said. "Sookan used it for letter practice."

"Look again," he said, holding the paper in front of her face again. "Look at number three," he said. "The ghost answered that one."

Jesse's last question was "Who was king of England in 1713?"

"In 1713?" Kate sat up and tried to clear her head. "What's so special about 1713?"

He shrugged. "I don't know," he said. "I just picked a year. I was running out of ideas. Look at what's next to the number."

Kate took the paper and looked at it more closely. In red crayon, beside question three were two letters—the only letters on the page that were neither O's nor H's.

"AN?" she said, handing it back to Jesse and getting out of bed. "That's some answer. Good old King An. I remember him well." She headed for the bathroom. "Did he come after or before King Arthur?"

"I just looked it up," Jesse yelled after her. "There was no king of England in 1713. There was a queen. And her name was—?" He paused, waiting for Kate's brain to start clicking.

Kate stopped and turned back to her brother. "Queen Anne?" she asked, stepping back into the room. "Isn't Queen Anne the kind of doll—?" She would have said more, but Jesse was running down the hall.

"Hey, Mom!" he called out. "Look at this!"

8

Queen Anne

"I know it's past the deadline, but there's been a problem with the printer."

The children closed the front door quietly, hearing the anxious tone in their mother's voice as she spoke on the phone in the kitchen.

"No, not my office printer—the printing company you hired for the project. The proofs aren't coming out right. The color's wrong. I've got to change the master to get it right. It's going to take more time."

As they approached the kitchen, the children could hear the angry voice, although not the words, coming from the other end of the phone.

"Within the week, I would think," Mrs. Spencer said after a pause. "It's not as simple as it sounds." Another pause. "I'll be in touch with you as soon as I can get it fixed."

She hung up the phone and then noticed the children in the doorway.

"Hi!" she said. That bright, phony tone was back. "How was school?"

"Problems, Mom?" Jesse asked.

"Oh, not really. Just a minor hitch." She glanced back at the telephone.

Kate began biting at her fingernail.

"But, speaking of problems," said their mother, "there's going to be a problem if you kids keep going online without permission."

"Online? Not me." Jesse looked at Kate. "Have you been online?"

"Nope," said Kate. "Not since your homework fiasco. Sookan?"

"Nope," said Sookan.

"Well, somebody has left the computer on an auction Web site twice," said Mrs. Spencer. "I know I didn't, so it must have been one of you."

"Or the ghost," said Kate.

"Pah-rahn Agah-si." Sookan grinned and nodded.

"There is no such thing as a ghost," Mrs. Spencer said firmly. Then, less firmly, she said, "And even if there is, what would the ghost want with an auction site?"

Jesse thought a minute. "We keep finding the doll in front of the computer. Maybe Pah-rahn Agah-si wants us to sell the doll on an auction site."

"I've been doing some research on our doll," Mrs. Spencer said.

"Shouldn't you be working on the color for that design?" Kate asked.

"I'll get the printer problem straightened out, Kate. Please don't worry about it. I had a little time left this afternoon while I was waiting for a call back, so I did some research. I found a good Web site about antique dolls."

"How much can we get for it?" Jesse asked, cutting to the important part.

"Well," his mother said, "it depends on when it was made. If it's really as old as it looks, it might be a Queen Anne."

"Made during the reign of Queen Anne, right?" Kate said.

"In 1713," said Jesse.

"How on earth did you know that, dear?" asked his mother.

Jesse shrugged. "Been studying," he said.

"Wonderful!" said his mother. "What else do you know about Queen Anne's time, Jesse?"

"Uhhhh," he said, biting his lower lip in thought. "They wore long dresses?"

"Lovely," said his mother. "The things the schools cover today are amazing. Really, I don't think I learned anything about the English throne till high school. Or maybe it was college. Well, anyway," she went on, "it's even possible that the doll could be really valuable. Turns out some of the dolls people call Queen Anne were made before Queen Anne came to power.

And, of course, some were made after she died, but they still call them Queen Annes."

"Which is ours?" Kate asked.

"Ah. That's the thing. Some that are called Queen Anne dolls really should be called William and Mary dolls. There are, according to the guy I found through the Web site, only about thirty of those in existence, and they're all in museums."

"Not in barn rafters, huh?" Jesse grinned.

"Well," Mrs. Spencer said, "it's possible. If our doll was made before 1700, it's a William and Mary, and the last one of those brought fifty thousand dollars at auction. That was several years ago."

"Wow!" said Jesse.

"Nice, huh?" his mother went on. "And another one of the authorities on the Internet said that if a real William and Mary–era doll was found, it would be priceless."

"Does priceless mean it isn't worth anything?" Jesse asked.

"No, that's what worthless means. Priceless means that it's so rare that it could be worth a lot."

"They should call it worthful then," said Jesse. "Or priceful."

"You can't change the English language, Jesse," Kate said.

"Well, somebody should," he said. "It doesn't make sense."

"Priceless will do fine. We'll be rich!" Kate said. "We could move back to Brooklyn!"

"Well, maybe not rich, but it sure would ease things up here for a while," Mrs. Spencer said.

Kate's smile disappeared instantly. "What about your big contract, Mom?"

"Well, there's been a shakeup at that company, and now they're not sure they want to go ahead with the project," her mother said. Then came the phony smile and voice. "Something else will turn up. I've got lots of feelers out there. Don't worry. And there's the doll, don't forget. I wonder where I put that doll expert's card."

"What if it's newer?" Kate said. "What if it's from after 1700?"

"Well, then it's only worth a thousand or so."

"A thousand dollars is still a lot of money," Kate said.

"Let's hope for the big bucks," said Mrs. Spencer. "We could use some."

"How much trouble are we in, Mom?" Kate asked, her fingernail back near her teeth.

Sookan paused with the spoon halfway to her mouth.

"Oh, not much, really," said their mother, trying and failing to wipe the worried look off her face. "It's going to be all right, kids. Really, it'll be all right, but doll money would surely help. We need to find out what the doll is worth. I've got to go to Manhattan tomorrow. I'll find the card and take the doll with me and get it appraised."

Kate sighed. "Manhattan," she said wistfully. "Just over the bridge from Brooklyn. Home. Can we go?"

"Not this time," said her mother. "It's a school day, remember? Come help me find that card."

Mrs. Spencer's office showed her typical lack of organization. Big piles of printouts and books threatened to topple at a touch. Framed photographs of the kids peeked out from the bottom of two of the piles. The pencil holder Kate had made for her in second grade was lying on its side with markers spilling out onto another pile of papers. An empty box labeled "Paper Clips" lay beside it.

Mrs. Spencer looked around as if noticing the mess for the first time. "Uh," she said. "It's here somewhere."

Kate and Jesse tried to organize the piles

as they searched. It was some time before Jesse said, "Here it is."

Kate took the card and read: "Antique Doll Appraisals, 263 East 57th St., New York, NY, 212-624-3047."

"Funny," Mrs. Spencer said. "You'd think it would give the person's name. Just an address and phone number. Oh, well," she said, placing the card in her purse. "That'll do."

Their mother was still in New York when the kids got home from school the next afternoon.

"Wouldn't it be great if it turns out to be a William and Mary doll?" Jesse said as they put down their backpacks and went into the kitchen.

"Nope," said Sookan. "Wrong one."

"You keep saying that," Kate said.

"No." Sookan grinned. "Sometimes I say *"Ee-guh aniya."*

"Yeah, yeah, very funny," said her sister. "But you don't know for sure that it's the wrong one, Sookan. It could be really valuable, and we need that money. Without it we'll never get back to Brooklyn."

"Brooklyn nothing," Jesse said. "Without it, we may not even be able to stay here."

Sookan pulled a stepstool over to the pantry shelf to take down the peanut butter.

"Mom's really worried no matter what she's telling us. She doesn't even sing lately, Kate," Jesse went on, getting out the glasses.

"Yeah," Kate said. "Never thought I'd miss those dumb songs." She took a loaf of bread from the refrigerator and handed the carton of milk to Jesse. "Wish there was something we could do to help," she said.

"I'm working on it," he said. "I've got to come up with a plan to use the ghost for answers."

"Got to hunt," Sookan said.

"Hunt? What for? Buried treasure?" Jesse asked.

Sookan grinned and shook her head. "Not buried, silly." She took a swig of milk, grabbed her sandwich, and headed out the back door. "Got to hunt."

Mrs. Spencer arrived about seven, looking exhausted.

"Any good news, Mom?" Jesse asked.

"Yep," she said. "I got a line on a couple more contracts."

"What about the doll?" Jesse asked. "Did you go to the shop on the card?"

"Yes, but it was closed," Mrs. Spencer said. "Funny little place. I had to call Mr. Jacobinski to get the name of another expert."

"Is it a William and Mary?" Kate asked.

Sookan shook her head and muttered, *"Ee-guh aniya."*

"Well, no," said their mother as Sookan

102

nodded. "This doll expert said it's not. Turns out to be a replica of a Queen Anne —probably made in the early 1900s, she said."

"How much is it worth?"

"Every little bit helps, dear. The expert thinks we should offer it on eBay. He says we could get a couple of hundred for it." She hurried toward the kitchen, speaking over her shoulder as she went. "Let me see what I can rustle up for dinner."

"So, the doll's a loser," Jesse said that night. "Time to get back to the ghost—it will answer some questions and not others. All I have to do is figure out which questions it will answer and we're rich. Maybe we really could afford to move back to Brooklyn."

"Brooklyn," Kate said dreamily. She looked down, and the dark gray floorboards under the table became polished hardwood. A small oriental rug appeared at her feet.

She could almost hear Lizzie's voice calling her to come outside for a game of Fifty Scatter.

"Brooklyn," echoed her mother. She imagined her hand holding a coffee mug as she stood in a busy office filled with colleagues and expensive computer equipment.

"Brooklyn," Jesse repeated, and the plate of macaroni and cheese in front of him seemed to change to one filled with potato salad, a dill pickle, and corned beef on rye with hot mustard from the deli down the street.

"More, please," said Sookan. She held her plate out to her mother, and they all snapped back to reality.

9

A Good One

The next Saturday morning, Sookan took a flashlight from the kitchen drawer and turned to Jesse and Kate. "C'mon," she said.

"Sure, go play," said their mother. "I've got work to do."

"Uh, where are we going, Sookan?" Jesse asked as Sookan led the way out the back door.

"Find a good one," she said.

"We're looking for a good one?" Kate asked. They walked along the side of the house, heading toward the back.

"Yep," Sookan said confidently.

"A good what?" asked Jesse.

"Yep!" Sookan said.

Kate and Jesse looked at each other and shrugged. Sookan knelt to examine the area around a cellar window, running her hand along the cement.

"Uh, Sookan," Jesse said, "can you tell us a bit more about this 'good one'?"

Sookan looked at her brother with her right eyebrow raised.

"Now, that's not fair, Sookan! Look, Kate, she can raise her eyebrow. How come I can't raise my eyebrow and you two can?" He twisted up his face, trying and failing to raise either eyebrow independently.

Kate looked at him and laughed, her eyebrow raised. Sookan was paying them no attention at all as she continued her search at the next window.

"Uh, Sookan," Jesse asked, "how will we know when we've found this good one?"

Sookan smiled broadly. "You go that way," she said to Jesse, pointing along the side of the house with her flashlight. "Agah-sis this way." She took Kate's hand and headed toward the cellar door.

"Agah-sis?" Kate pulled back as Sookan

106

opened the door. "Does *agah-si*s mean 'girl,' Sookan?"

"More," Sookan said. "C'mon."

"Girls?"

"Bigger." She held her hand up higher than her head.

"Bigger? Older than girls?" Kate asked.

"Yep."

"Women?"

Sookan nodded.

"And *pah-rahn* means 'blue'?"

Sookan smiled broadly.

"Hey, Jesse!" Kate called out. "*Pah-rahn agah-si* means 'blue woman.'"

"Fascinating!" Jesse called back. "Hey, there's a snakeskin here. Come look."

"Nope! C'mon, Kate." Sookan pulled her sister toward the cellar.

"Sookan, let's sit out here in the sunshine, and you can teach me some more Korean words. Won't that be fun?" Kate said. She thought her voice sounded very much like her mother's phony one.

107

Sookan looked at her with a raised eyebrow.

"Oh, dear," Kate said, and followed her sister down the dark cellar stairs.

"Have fun, agah-sis!" Jesse called from the next cellar window.

"Oh, Sookan," Kate said, looking around the dark cellar. "Can't we switch?"

Sookan turned on the flashlight and shone it in Kate's face.

"See, it's like this, Sookan," Kate explained, shading her eyes from the beam. "The cellar's really creepy, and Jesse likes creepy places. So, let's switch and Jesse can come down here, and you and I can watch him through the window, okay?" She tried her mother's phony smile. As long as she sounded like her mother, she might as well look like her too. "Won't that be fun?"

"Nope," said Sookan. "C'mon."

The light from the open cellar door allowed a few feet of visibility, and there was a small amount of light from the windows. Sookan headed into the darker area of the cellar without hesitation, the flashlight giving out its narrow beam ahead of her. Kate approached cautiously. Their mother's cleaning sessions hadn't taken on the cellar yet. Kate had been glad of that, but now she wished for the clean walls and windows such a session would have left behind.

The floor was dirt and gave off a dank and moldy smell. What if previous owners of the house had buried something awful here, Kate thought—like bodies, maybe? Almost immediately something wrapped itself around Kate's face. She screamed, grabbing at it frantically before she realized it was the string from a light bulb overhead.

"Okay?" Sookan's flashlight beam shone back from the darkness. Kate pulled on the light string, and the bare bulb gave off a precious sixty watts of light.

"Yeah," Kate said weakly. "I'm okay." A

long rickety table ran along the wall next to the furnace. It seemed a safe enough place to start her search. Kate bent to examine the shelf that ran along the bottom of it. Strange dusty and rust-encrusted shapes lay scattered along the shelf. Gingerly, she reached for one and stood to hold it up to the light.

A loud rap on the window made her scream again, and she dropped the object with a thud.

"Find anything?" Jesse yelled in.

"I don't know," Kate shouted back. "I found an old jigsaw, I think. Is that what we're looking for, Sookan?" she asked into the darkness as she picked it up.

"Nope!" Sookan's cheerful voice came back. "Silly."

Kate put the jigsaw back on the shelf.

"Lookit!" Sookan called out a few minutes later. She handed the flashlight to Kate, who shone it first toward Sookan, then in the direction Sookan pointed. An object lay in the dirt at the back corner of the cellar floor.

"Looks like an old knife," Kate said, picking it up with the thumb and forefinger of her right hand.

"Yep! Good one." Sookan led the way out of the cellar.

They blinked in the daylight as they came up the cellar stairs.

10

The Knife

"Hey! Cool!" Jesse said when he saw the knife. He took it from Kate and brushed away some of the caked-on dirt. With a few layers of dirt removed, you could see a sort of rope-like pattern on the handle. The blade of the knife was encased in a leather sheath edged in metal. Kate carefully pulled it from the sheath to reveal a wide single-edged blade about six inches long.

"Read it," said Sookan, speaking over her shoulder as she walked into the house.

"Read it?" Jesse looked at Kate. "How do you read a knife?"

"Sookan's got her English mixed up. She probably means look at it." Kate handed the knife to Jesse and followed her sister inside. "Don't cut yourself. Show it to Mom."

"Think it's valuable?" he asked, putting the blade back in the sheath and going in behind them.

"Who knows?" Kate shrugged.

"Little bit," Sookan said.

"Oh, sure. The Korean knife expert speaks," Jesse said. "Hey, Mom! Look what Sookan found!" He and Kate headed toward the office. Sookan went upstairs.

Mrs. Spencer held her index finger toward them as she spoke into the phone at her desk. "Well," she said. "I'm sorry about that. Perhaps you'll think of me next time you have a similar project in mind." She hung up the phone and stared at it for a moment. Then she drew a deep breath and turned her attention toward the object Jesse held out. "What have you got there?" she asked. She was back to her phony self again.

"Trouble, Mom?" Kate asked.

"No, not really," she said. "Just another dead end."

Jesse handed her the knife. "Sookan found this in the cellar, Mom. Can I have it?"

"Sookan found it?" his mother asked, looking around him for her younger daughter. "Where is she?"

"Upstairs," Jesse said. "She doesn't want it. She said 'Read it,' but she means look at it. She's too young for a knife anyway. Can I have it? I'll be really careful, Mom. Looks like a pirate's knife, doesn't it? It'll be good for cutting branches."

"Well, for goodness sake." Mrs. Spencer examined the handle before slowly drawing the knife from its sheath. She peered closely at the blade. "Read it, huh? Where's your magnifying glass, Kate?"

Kate went off to find it.

"Can I have it, Mom?" Jesse asked again.

"No, dear," she said. "It's not a toy. It's too dangerous, and I think it's really old."

"Why do you need the magnifying glass? Eyes going, Mom? You're getting up there,

114

you know. Pushing forty."

"My eyes are just fine, thank you very much, Jesse," said his mother. "And I'm a long way from forty." Jesse tried and failed to raise his eyebrow. "Well, all right. A short way. But there's something written on the blade," she said.

"'This knife belongs to Jesse Spencer,' maybe," he said. "Is it worth a lot of money, do you think?"

Kate was back with the magnifying glass.

"I thought so," their mother said as she took the knife over by the desk lamp. "It *has* got writing on the blade. *'No me saques sin razón. No me emvaines sin honor,'*" she read.

"Korean?" Jesse asked, peering over her shoulder at the barely decipherable writing.

"Spanish," she said. "And, if I remember my college Spanish correctly, it says, 'Do not—*saques*—take me out—draw—do not draw me without reason. Do not—

cover me?—sheath me without honor.' Sounds like a noble motto."

Kate was looking directly at Jesse. "Sookan said, 'Read it.'"

"How'd she know it had writing on it?"

"Spooky, huh?"

"Blue Woman?" Jesse offered.

Kate shrugged. "She sure knew where to look for it."

"Well, get her to ask Blue Woman how much it's worth, then," Jesse said. "Maybe it's big bucks, Mom."

"Wouldn't that be nice, Jesse. See what you can find out about Spanish knives on the Internet, kids," she said. "And check out those books on antiques on the bottom shelf. There may be something in them about Spanish knives. I've got to make some calls." She reached for the phone as Jesse and Kate sat down in front of the computer. Then she seemed to change her mind. "I'll use the phone in the kitchen."

"She doesn't want us to hear," Kate said

when her mother had left the room.

"Things are really going down the tubes, aren't they, Kate?"

Kate nodded. "I think so," she said. She began to bite her nail again.

"Think we're going to lose this house too?" he asked.

Kate didn't want to think about that. "Let's hope this knife is worth a fortune. Try 'Spanish knives,'" she said as the search engine appeared on the screen.

11

Ghostly Tricks

They found a knife with the same description as theirs, including the motto on the blade, at an auction site. It was listed as a Cuban knife, a souvenir from the Spanish-American War. The highest bid on the one offered for sale was $1,000. Mrs. Spencer put their knife and the doll up for bid.

"Cross your fingers, kids," she said.

During the next few weeks Sookan continued to hunt, enlisting Jesse and Kate's help whenever she could, but found nothing.

Then came the attic. They hadn't even realized that there was one. There was no stairway leading to it, but one day Jesse was on the second floor of the barn when he looked across at the house. He noticed a window up at the very peak in the back.

"If there's a window, we've got to be able to reach it," he said, and began searching for a way to get up there. "C'mon, Sookan. Help us find the secret stairway. There may be real treasure up there."

"Yeah," Kate said. "It's a great title for a story. 'Dirk Blood and the Secret Attic.'"

"Nope," Sookan said. *"Ee-guh aniya."*

"In the attic?" Kate asked.

"Yep," said Sookan.

It was Kate who spotted the trapdoor in the ceiling of the linen closet. They had to drag the stepladder from the kitchen up to the second floor, and Kate pulled the strap that hung from the door. It stuck at first, but after a couple of hard pulls the door swung open, and a rope ladder dropped down, its bottom step about six inches above the closet floor.

"You first," Kate said.

Jesse scrambled up, needing no further encouragement.

"Hey! Cool!" he said.

"See anything yucky?" Kate called up to him.

"Nothing moving. It's safe. Come on up," Jesse said, and Kate climbed up the ladder.

"Be careful up there, you two," Mrs. Spencer cautioned. She climbed up herself and looked around. "I guess it's okay," she said. "Have fun, kids. I'm going back to work."

It was hot in the small attic room. The single tiny window provided the only light. It was completely empty except for a trunk under the window.

"Open it," Jesse said.

"Oh, no," Kate said, stepping back. "There may be things living in there. You open it."

Jesse shrugged and unlatched the lid. "Girls!" he said as he looked inside. "Nothing to be scared of here. No treasure either. Just old clothes."

Kate knelt to see for herself. On top was a dark pink hat with a broad brim. Badly crushed artificial flowers circled the crown of the hat, and two ribbons dangled down from each side. She put it aside and took out the dress beneath it. It was made of pink material that seemed to be some sort of satin. There was lace that must once have been white around the neck. Kate stood and held it up under her chin.

"Wow!" Jesse said. "You can wear it for Halloween, Kate. Bet it would fit."

Kate quickly pulled the dress on over her T-shirt and shorts.

The skirt was long and full. She put on the hat and tied the ribbons under her chin.

"How do I look?" she said. "I feel like someone in a movie."

"Take it off," Jesse said.

"Why?"

"Kate," he said in a quavering voice, "you look like wallpaper."

"Wallpaper?" Kate was puzzled for a moment, then she gasped. She snatched off the hat and dress and stuffed them back into the trunk. She slammed it shut. Jesse was already down the ladder, and it didn't take Kate long to get down either. Jesse climbed the stepladder and flung the rope ladder back into the attic, shutting the trapdoor behind them.

"*Ee-guh aniya,*" Sookan said.

"Well," Jesse said shakily, "I don't think we need to search the attic any more."

"Right," said Kate, her eyes as wide as Jesse's. "We're finished with the attic. Let's head back to the barn."

Mrs. Spencer checked the auction site daily, and the bids came slowly until the last three days of the offer. Then the bids on the doll went from $200 to $350, where they stopped. Bids on the knife were better but followed the same pattern, going from $475 to $1,200 at the last minute.

"Maybe I'll be an antique dealer if writing, ornithology, and mineralogy don't work out," Kate said. She also thought she might make a valuable antique the motive for murder in her next Dirk Blood adventure. Maybe she could have an antique dealer as one of the suspects.

"Not bad," their mother said as she accepted the bids and made arrangements to ship the doll and the knife to the buyers. "Add treasure hunter to your career list, Kate. Fifteen hundred and fifty dollars minus the Web site fee pays the mortgage and some of the other bills for the month. That takes the heat off for now. Congratulations, kids!" She walked into the office singing, *"Every time it rains it rains pennies from heaven."*

Sookan looked at Kate and Jesse with a wide grin. "Singing!" she said, nodding her head toward her departing mother. Sookan held both thumbs up and then started out the door. "Got to hunt."

"Nice to have Mom singing again, isn't it, Jesse?" Kate said.

123

But Jesse was frowning. "For a month?" he said. "It only pays the bills for a month, Kate. What do we do about the next month?"

"I don't know," she said, "but I think we go with Sookan. She found the knife, after all."

"I found the doll," Jesse said. "How come you're not following me?"

"Because you're not going anywhere," Kate said.

"There's gotta be a way to use that ghost," he said.

"Well, you keep thinking," Kate said. "I'm going hunting with Sookan."

Sookan was practicing her letters at the kitchen table that evening, the tip of her tongue sticking out of the corner of her mouth. She pronounced each letter as she drew it.

Mrs. Spencer was at the computer in her

office, and Kate was in the bathroom upstairs. Jesse, doing his homework at the dining room table, could hear the shower running. Suddenly he felt very cold. He looked down at his hand to see that the blue light was shining on it. He wanted to shake it off, but his hand felt so cold that he could barely move it.

"Hey!" he shouted. "Mom! Kate?" He dropped the pencil and jumped up, shaking his hand in the air before tucking it under his armpit to warm it up. "Hey! Sookan? Somebody?"

Sookan kept on working. The light was no longer on his hand when he drew it out from under his arm. The light was moving across the room. Jesse followed it into the kitchen in time to see it disappear into the kitchen wall.

"Cute!" he said, addressing his remarks to the spot on the wall where the light had disappeared. "If you've got nothing better to do, why don't you do my homework?"

"Can't," Sookan said, looking up. "Writing."

"I'm not talking to you, Sookan. I'm talking to the—light," he said, his voice fading as Sookan smiled at him.

He sat down at the dining room table and waited. When nothing else happened, he picked up his pencil and went back to work.

A few minutes later, Kate shouted down from upstairs, "Hey! I'm taking a shower here! Who's running the hot water down there?"

She came down the stairs wrapped in a towel and walked quickly to the office where their mother was working.

Mrs. Spencer looked up. "You're dripping all over the carpet."

"Jesse used up all the hot water, Mom, and I was in the middle of a shower."

"Me?" Jesse exclaimed. "I didn't do anything to the water. I'm doing my homework. Right, Sookan?"

"All right, Jesse. That's not funny. I'm freezing," Kate said. "And look at my hair!" Her hair was dripping soapsuds, and a puddle of water was forming on the rug.

Jesse said, "I haven't moved. Honest! Have I, Sookan?" He looked over at Sookan, who had her eyebrow raised. "Well, all right, I moved, but I didn't do anything to the water. Did I, Sookan?"

Sookan shook her head.

"Well, all of a sudden the water turned icy cold."

"It's the ghost," Jesse declared. "It's playing tricks tonight. It turned my hand blue and made me drop the pencil."

"Enough about the blue light," said their mother. "The blue light is just the sunlight shining through the blue window. It's not a ghost. It can't do anything."

"Uh, Mom," Jesse said. "It's night. The sun went down some time ago."

"Is it that late already?" his mother said. She thought a moment. "Well, it's head-lights going by on the road and reflecting through the blue window."

Kate and Sookan each raised one eyebrow at her while Jesse tried in vain to do the same.

"What's your explanation for my shower going from warm to icy cold? You can't claim that the sun and the headlights did that." Kate wiped a glob of soapsuds from her forehead and continued to shiver.

"Well, that," said her mother decisively, "is easily explained. The supply of hot water is not endless, Kate. You took too long a shower, and the hot water ran out."

"How about the cold?" asked Jesse. "My hand turned to ice, Mom, when the light shone on it. Really. You should have seen it. Sookan saw it. Didn't you, Sookan?"

Sookan shook her head. "Reading," she said.

"It's just your imagination, Jesse," Mrs. Spencer declared. "Suggestibility is a very powerful thing. You associate the blue light with cold, and you saw the blue light and felt cold. It's as simple as that."

"I see," said Jesse. "Would you care to explain the answers to the mountain measuring and the queen of England thing, Mom?"

"The open book is a coincidence, and the letters were Sookan's," she said.

"And the TV?" Kate asked. "The television set only goes off when the ghost wants it to. Explain that, Dr. Wizard."

"I can," Mrs. Spencer declared. "This is an old house and the wiring needs replacing. It makes connections and then, when it gets heated, it sometimes loses the connection." She looked very proud of her solution. "As soon as we can afford it, we'll have all the wiring replaced, and that problem will be solved. You'd better get dressed, Kate. You'll catch your death of cold."

"And how do you expect me to get this shampoo out of my hair?" Kate asked as she stomped back up the stairs.

"Cold water is refreshing!" Jesse called after her.

Later, they sat down to watch TV together. "Where's the remote?" their mother asked, checking around the coffee table where they usually kept it.

"Here," Sookan said. She came in from the kitchen with the remote in her hand.

"Why did you take it into the kitchen?" Jesse asked. "You can't turn on the TV from there."

"Not me," Sookan said. She smiled broadly. "Pah-rahn Agah-si."

"Now why would she do a thing like that?" Mrs. Spencer asked. "Why would she want the remote control?"

"Who?" Jesse and Kate asked at the same time.

"Never mind," Mrs. Spencer said. "Hand it to me, Sookan. Let's see if there's anything good on."

Much later, a very sleepy, very cranky Sookan came stomping down the stairs.

The others watched as, without a word, she went into the kitchen and came out carrying her pillow. "Pah-rahn Agah-si," she said by way of explanation, and she went back upstairs to bed.

"What on earth is going on here?" Mrs. Spencer asked as she retrieved her appointment book from the kitchen counter after searching the house for it an hour or so later. "Whoever's doing this is going to lose some privileges if they don't stop."

"Wonder what privileges she can take away from a ghost," Jesse said.

"Okay," Kate said. "I give up, Pah-rahn Agah-si. There's no point in trying to get anything done here tonight. You do your stuff, and we'll just stay right here and watch."

They sat at the kitchen table watching the counter and the doorway, but after a half hour, when nothing moved and nothing new appeared on the kitchen counter, they gave up and went to bed.

12

Disaster

The school year was over. Both Kate and Jesse were glad to see it end. It had been a tough year. They hoped some kids would move into town over the summer so that next year Kate and Jesse wouldn't be the new kids anymore.

The family wouldn't be able to afford a real vacation this year, but Mrs. Spencer suggested that they all go with her into New York for a day. She had an appointment on Madison Avenue that she was sure wouldn't take long. She could drop them off at the old neighborhood, and they could visit Keith and Lizzie.

"Need to hunt," Sookan protested.

"C'mon, Sookan," Jesse pleaded. "It'll be fun. I can't wait to see Keith. Wait till he hears about the ghost. He'll go nuts!"

"I'm bringing my new story to read to Lizzie. She'll love it," Kate said. "'Dirk Blood and the Bloody Knife.'"

"One day away from this place will do us all good," Mrs. Spencer said.

Sookan whispered, "Need to hunt," but she climbed into the car with her family when it was time to go.

It was fun for Jesse and Kate to get back to their old neighborhood, and Sookan dutifully looked at whatever her brother and sister pointed out of interest on the way. They grew more and more excited as they got closer.

Lizzie and Keith and some other friends gathered quickly in front of the old brownstone, and they were all very glad to see one another, but it seemed awkward. Nobody knew what to say or where to look, and conversation was rough going. Neither Keith nor Lizzie seemed to care much about their friends' lives in Massachusetts.

Interest perked up when Jesse began to

talk about the ghost, but no one believed him even when Kate and Sookan swore it was true. It was hard for Kate and Jesse to listen to what their friends' school year had been like. Sookan, not having any friends in the city, just waited patiently.

Jesse suggested a game of Fifty Scatter, but Lizzie said she had a ballet lesson, and Keith was supposed to meet some friends for a movie.

They got lunch at the corner deli, and the corned beef sandwiches were just as good as they remembered. They had Italian ice for dessert from Mr. Cimini's stand, but Kate and Jesse were relieved when their mother came to pick them up.

It was a quiet ride home. Kate was disappointed that Lizzie and she had not picked up their friendship right where it left off, but she was sure that if she moved back to the city, they'd quickly be best friends again. Who would have thought that Lizzie would be interested in ballet?

As they drove down their road in Massachusetts, Kate thought back to that first morning, how they'd all cried when they saw the house. Even now it looked pretty discouraging. All their redecorating time and money had been spent on the inside of the house. The gray paint was peeling off the clapboards and the faded blue shutters were hardly inviting. It would look better when they could afford to repaint the outside, Kate thought—maybe a light yellow with white shutters.

"Come on, Sookan," Jesse said when she seemed to hesitate in getting out of the car. "There's still enough daylight to swing. I'll push you for a while."

"I'm going to see if the swifts are back at the pond," Kate said.

But Sookan's eyes were wide and her face was solemn as she climbed out of the car. "No," she said. "Got to go in."

They could hear the sound of water dripping as they opened the front door.

"Now what?" their mother asked as they hurried into the kitchen.

Water was cascading down the kitchen wall between the stove and refrigerator. The plaster was soaked through, and big chunks had fallen to the floor, which was flooded with a couple of inches of water. There was a big hole in the wall.

They all stood and stared. Then Mrs. Spencer grabbed a flashlight and headed down to the cellar. "Come on, Jesse," she said. "Help me find the shut-off valve. Kate, call the plumber. The number's on the pad by the telephone. Sookan, go get all the towels from the linen closet and the mop."

The plumber promised to come first thing in the morning. It was late in the evening when the last of the water and the plaster were off the counters and the floor.

They stood there exhausted, surveying the damage. The hole in the wall was even bigger now, as more cakes of sodden plaster had fallen off while they worked.

"Whew!" said Jesse. "Do you think the ghost did that?"

"It was no ghost," said his mother. "Just an old pipe giving out. Of all the cursed luck!" She looked around, and the enormity of it seemed to hit her. "This we didn't need. Look at it!" She waved her arms. "We'll have to replace that whole wall. The plumber's going to cost a fortune. What are we going to do?" She burst into tears and hurried from the room.

The children stared after her.

"You know," said Jesse, anxious to think about something besides his mother's tears, "that hole is right where the ghost disappears each time. Bet Pah-rahn Agah-si got really soaked when the pipe burst. Wonder if the water put out the blue light." He climbed up on the kitchen counter and stuck his head into the hole. "Hey! This is cool, guys! Look at all these pipes."

The last thing Kate wanted to see was a

water pipe, but Sookan climbed up on the counter beside her brother. She stuck her upper body through the hole and then pointed. "Lookit! Over there," she said.

"Over where?" Jesse asked. She nudged him out of the way and leaned into the hole so far her feet came off the counter. More plaster caked off onto the counter.

"Hey! Be careful, Sookan!" Kate called, dashing over to grab her sister's feet. "You'll fall in! And we don't need to make more mess here."

Sookan pulled back out of the hole, holding something in her right hand. She held it up triumphantly. "Right one!" she called out.

13

The Right One

"Well, I'll be darned," Mrs. Spencer said when she saw the second doll. Her eyes and nose were red, but, to their relief, she was no longer crying. "There was another doll, after all."

"Agatha Paran said there was more treasure," Kate said. "How did she know that?"

"Sookan said so too," Jesse reminded them.

The second doll looked even worse than the first one had. What clothes were on it were moldy and blackened. It had a wooden head and a cloth body and jointed wooden legs and arms. Mrs. Spencer gently brushed off a bit of dirt from the face with her forefinger to reveal a painted eye that seemed to stare back.

"Sookan told us the other one was the

wrong one," said Jesse. "How did you know that, Sookan?"

Sookan slowly raised one eyebrow.

"Now quit that," Jesse said. "Did the blue woman tell you?"

Sookan just smiled and shrugged.

"Well, if she did, say thank you for us," Kate said.

"Hey!" Jesse remembered. "That's why the light was going crazy that night, bringing all those things into that side of the kitchen. It was trying to lead us to the kitchen wall."

"I'm not so sure it wasn't someone else playing a bit of a joke," Mrs. Spencer said, looking closely at her children as she spoke.

"Think we can get as much for this doll as we did the other one, Mom?" Jesse asked after an uneasy silence.

"I don't know," said his mother. "Could be. It certainly looks as old as that one."

"More," said Sookan. "Right one this time."

"Well, only an expert can tell us for sure," Mrs. Spencer said.

"Right one this time," Sookan repeated.

"One expert heard from," her mother said, "but I think we need a second opinion."

"Going to try Mr. Jacobinski's first expert?" Kate asked.

"It's easier to get to," Mrs. Spencer answered. "Might as well start there."

In New York, after circling the area a few times, Mrs. Spencer found a parking spot only a few blocks away from the doll shop.

"One thing about living in the country," she said as she maneuvered into the space. "Parking isn't such a problem."

"That parking garage was much closer," Kate said.

"Too expensive," her mother said. "A meter will do fine. We won't be long and the walk will do us good."

New York was having a bad air day, and it

took the children a few minutes to adjust to the heat and haze that hit them as they climbed out of the car.

"Yeah," Kate said. "Nothing like a brisk walk in the smog."

"Yuck!" Jesse said, blinking his eyes.

"The joys of the city," his mother said, putting coins in the meter before leading the way up the street.

"Forgot about this stuff," Kate said.

Sookan sniffed and grinned. "Better at home," she said.

"The air's better across the bridge in Brooklyn," Kate said. "It isn't usually like this. Is it, Jesse?"

"Nah," he said, but his tone said otherwise.

The doll appraiser's shop was tucked between a cigar store and a curtain shop. A hand-painted sign over the door said simply "Doll Place." Most of the display window was covered with posters and signs advertising doll exhibits and sales, some of which dated from one or two years before. The only object visible through the glass was a large dollhouse.

The children shaded their eyes with their hands for a better look. Hearing their gasps, Mrs. Spencer shaded her own eyes and peered in. The house was a replica of their own in Massachusetts, complete with a bedroom with the doll wallpaper.

Wide-eyed, they turned toward the door, where a faded cardboard sign said "Open 9–5." A bell tinkled as they walked inside. The light was dim, and it took a minute before they spotted the woman standing behind the counter.

They stared at her, speechless.

"Welcome," Agatha Paran said calmly. "You're late." She was dressed in a bright blue smock that seemed to sparkle even in the dim light. She reached out her hand and, without a word, Mrs. Spencer placed the second doll in it.

"Late? How can we be late?"

"Why didn't you tell us . . . ?"

"Did you put the doll in our wall?"

"How did you . . . ?"

"Where is . . . ?"

"Who . . . ?"

Jesse and Kate and their mother spoke at once as questions bubbled out, but Agatha Paran ignored them and examined the doll.

"Hello, my beauty," she said.

The questions continued, but the little woman paid them no mind. She placed the doll on a sheet of clean paper, took out a magnifying glass, and bent over it, carefully turning it this way and that.

Since their continued questions were no more successful than the first ones, the children went over to the dollhouse. From inside the shop they could see the exterior of the house, which was light gray with dark blue shutters. The door was natural oak with a brightly polished brass knocker.

"Would you all care to hear the final verdict?" Agatha Paran asked them at last.

"Of course," Mrs. Spencer said, and they all came over to her.

"It's the real thing," Agatha said, smiling.

"A William and Mary?" Kate asked.

"You bet." When the old woman smiled, the curves seemed to be echoed by all the wrinkles in her face.

"Worthless? I mean, priceless?" Jesse asked.

"Maybe not priceless," she said. "But I've a buyer that I know would give you one hundred thousand dollars for it."

"Sold!" Mrs. Spencer said.

"You might be able to get more at auction," Agatha cautioned.

"Family conference," Mrs. Spencer declared, motioning her children to a corner of the shop; but the "conference" consisted of speechless nods.

"We think we'll stick with you," Mrs. Spencer said firmly, "but I would like you to answer a few questions before we go."

"All in good time," Agatha said, "I'll answer all your questions in a minute. Just let me put this somewhere safe." She took the doll with her through a door in the back of the shop.

Jesse went back over to the dollhouse, and the others joined him. Through one tiny window they could see a very faint blinking blue light.

They rushed out the door to see it from the other side, but they could see no light. When they tried to go back inside the shop, they found the door had locked behind them.

They knocked and rattled the door handle, but no one came.

"She probably can't hear us from the back of the shop," Mrs. Spencer said. "She'll come in a minute."

They waited, at first patiently and then less so, as several minutes went by.

Kate said nervously, "She's got our doll!"

She began chewing on her thumbnail.

Jesse knocked on the door again. "Mrs. Paran! Let us in!" he called. "The door's locked!"

"Give us back our doll!" Kate yelled.

They knocked and then hammered at the door for a long time, but no one answered.

"She can't get away with that," Kate said. "Can she, Mom?"

"What'll we do?" Jesse asked.

"We'll get a policeman," Mrs. Spencer said. They started off down the street.

"Wait," Sookan said. She pointed to the bottom of the door as a check for $100,000 slowly slid out.

14

Decisions

They had to wait at their bank in Massachusetts to make sure there were enough funds in Mrs. Paran's account to cover the check. They waited nervously at the counter, but there was no problem. The teller came back with the deposit slip for $100,000.

That night they sat around the dining room table, finishing off the supper of potato salad and corned beef sandwiches with kosher dill pickles that they'd brought home from the deli.

"How do you think Agatha Paran knew there was another doll?" Kate asked. "Did she put it there? And what about that dollhouse? Wasn't that weird? How do you suppose she got it?"

"Maybe her father made it for her. She

said she always loved this place," Mrs. Spencer said.

"Is she keeping the doll herself or did she really have a buyer?" Kate asked.

"Who knows?" her mother said. "I don't think it matters much, does it?"

"She's always wearing blue," Jesse said. "That thing she was wearing today was almost shining." He paused a moment and then his eyes got bigger. "Hey, could she be the blue light?"

"Pah-rahn Agah-si—Agatha Paran. They sure sound alike," Kate said.

They all turned to Sookan, who was concentrating on her sandwich.

"Is she?" Jesse asked. "Is Agatha Paran your blue light, Sookan?"

"Not mine," she said. "Silly." Her eyes were twinkling.

"Well, is she the light that followed you from Korea? Is she some sort of guardian ghost?" Jesse said.

Sookan shrugged.

"Mom?" Kate asked. "Is she?"

"I doubt that we'll ever find out any of those things," Mrs. Spencer said. "I think our light is a mystery and Agatha Paran is a mystery and I think she likes it that way."

Kate said, "I'd sure like to have that dollhouse. Do you suppose she'd sell it, Mom? We can afford it now, can't we?"

"Well," Mrs. Spencer said as she wiped a smear of mustard off her cheek. "We might be able to afford it, but I'm not sure that's how we'll want to spend our money. I think we need a family conference to decide where the money goes."

"I vote for an allowance," Jesse said, licking the dregs of potato salad from the side of his lips.

Kate was staring at her mother. "Brooklyn?" she asked hesitantly.

Sookan looked up from her plate.

"Brooklyn's certainly a possibility now," said their mother. "We can't get our old brownstone back, of course, but maybe we could find a place in the same neighbor-hood."

"Writers' group," Kate said wistfully.

"I could maybe get my old job back," said their mother. "No more struggling for new contracts."

"Yeah," said Kate. "It would be nice not to worry." She might even be able to stop biting her nails, she thought, looking at her torn red cuticles.

"Deli," Jesse said. "Italian ice and the candy store and suppers like this any time we want them."

"People," Mrs. Spencer said. "It would be great to have people to work with again."

"Games of Fifty Scatter every night," said Jesse.

Kate nodded. "Every night," she agreed. "Friends again."

"Walking to school instead of those long school bus rides," reminded their mother. "You kids won't have to get up so early."

"Yeah," said Jesse. "But the bus was kind

of fun sometimes." He turned to Kate. "I thought you and Maria were friends."

"Yeah, kind of," Kate said.

"You sat together on the bus those last couple of weeks."

Kate nodded. "Maria's nice," she said. "She said she'd come over some day this summer. You've got friends here, though, Jesse. How about that fort you and those guys were building?"

"Yeah. We're trying to figure out how to put on a roof." He smiled. "Hey! Maybe we can get up a game of Fifty Scatter with those kids and Maria. There's lots of good places to hide here." He looked out the window. "All those trees back there, the barn, the cellar." He paused. "And the attic."

"That's one place where you won't have to look for me," Kate said, shivering slightly.

"Right!" he said. "Me neither."

Sookan had been very quiet, not even moving her head as her eyes darted around at her family. Now they all looked at her.

"How do you feel about moving back to Brooklyn, Sookan?" their mother asked.

"No barn in Brooklyn," she said.

"Yeah. The barn's nice," Kate said. "I still think there must be chiastolites somewhere in those rocks, and I was thinking of cleaning up one of the stables there. It would make a good studio—great place to write."

"'Dirk Blood meets Pah-rahn Agah-si,' huh?" Jesse said.

"You know, he could," Kate said. Her mind was racing along now. Dirk Blood could be hired to solve the mystery. Boy! He'd get some answers from Agatha Paran.

"No swing in Brooklyn," Sookan said, interrupting Kate's plotting.

"Well, we could maybe put a swing set in the back yard in Brooklyn," said their mother.

Sookan said, "No pond in Brooklyn."

"Yeah. The pond is great," admitted

Jesse. "I think I saw a big turtle on the other side of it this morning. Maybe it was a snapping turtle. You think there could be snapping turtles there, Mom?"

"Maybe," she said a little nervously.

"Bird watching is great around the pond," Kate said. "The herons are back."

"No Pah-rahn Agah-si in Brooklyn," Sookan said.

Everyone was quiet then as they thought of the on-and-off television, the cold, and the mysterious blue light.

"Things would be a bit less exciting," Mrs. Spencer said, not at all sure that wouldn't be a good thing. "Things might even stay where we put them."

"Maybe she'd come back with us," Kate said. "Maybe she'd help us find treasure in Brooklyn."

"No," said Sookan.

"Really?" said Jesse. "You don't think she'd come with us to Brooklyn, Sookan?"

"No," Sookan repeated. She looked

around at her family and then around the room. "She likes it here," she said.

"Well, maybe so, but we need to think about us. Where do we want to live?" said their mother. She peered out at the destroyed kitchen wall. "This place has its charms, but so does Brooklyn. Things seem less hectic in the city." She grinned as she thought that statement over. "Country life is supposed to be peaceful, isn't it?"

"Can we have both?" Jesse asked.

"No," said his mother. "We cannot. One hundred thousand dollars is a lot of money, but not enough for two houses. We could use the money to finish fixing up this place. Repair that wall and fix up the outside, even get these floors sanded."

Kate said, "No more ugly gray paint."

"That'd be nice," said Jesse.

"The thing to think about," their mother went on, "is which place feels like home."

They were all quiet for quite a while, lost in thought. As each one seemed to come to a decision, they looked at Sookan, who had a big smile on her face.

"Here?" she said, as if she knew the answer.

Without hesitation, they all nodded. "Here," they said.

"Good," said Sookan. "Let's swing."